The
Vice President
The $50 000 Club
Foreign Frights

Elina Salajeva

Created By

Elinadeivid

DISCLAIMER

This is a work of fiction. Names, characters, businesses, places, events, and incidents are either the products of the author's imagination or used in a fictitious manner. Any resemblance to actual persons, living or dead, or actual events is purely coincidental.

DEDICATION

To all the future leaders and all ambitious great minds

Touchladybirdlucky Studios

A David Gomadza Production.

ACKNOWLEDGMENTS

Many thanks and best wishes to the Elinadeivid brand. Big thanks also to Touchladybirdlucky Studios.

CHAPTER ONE

"I want to make it clear that gone are the days when these tycoons put profits first instead of human lives. Gone are the days when reckless and irresponsible behavior was tolerated. The world is changing, so as the goals and values in society. We as the young generations we are the future. We are the leaders of tomorrow, so as it is I want to emphasize that tomorrow begins today. We can no longer watch these CEO's grow their pockets big at our expense. We can't tolerate anymore a society where year after year these irresponsible people of generations gone by break records of weapons production at the expense of the future generations. Accountability begins today. It starts with us. As you have heard them yourself, they say it has never been done before and therefore it shall never be. But let me say this to you, ladies and gentlemen, and honorable people, we are the future generation. Let us decide what is right for us. What worked yesterday, we can't promise that,

that will work tomorrow. The future is for the young, but unfortunately as the way things are going they won't be any left. Weapons manufactured by these companies are claiming the future of tomorrow at an alarming rate while we stand aside and watch. They say that they have the money to buy everyone out. I ask you today, ladies and gentlemen; will their money ever replace the lives of the young ones they are claiming? Will their money ever replace the limbs they are claiming daily? As you know yourselves, no one will ever voice for them, not because they can't but because no one will listen. For some of you, maybe the car you drove today was made with the blood money that claimed lives. Maybe the house you live in, was built by the proceeds from weapons sale. The money you have in your pocket maybe was from they acted responsibly as they can't be held accountable for what happens after the sale has been completed. You will hear them swear by their bible, the Arms act, that under the law they are protected and are not answerable to anyone. But when it comes to selling weapons to international, often poor countries. I am going to argue that, they cannot make money without the assumed responsibilities toward the international community. They can't claim a lack of foresight or a lack of knowledge, that their weapons will end up in the wrong hands. This all amounts to negligence as they should reasonably foresee that their weapons might end up being used to kill children. Human lives matter more than local Arms acts and profits. They will argue that it is not their responsibility to ensure that weapons are used as stated in the agreement. Theoretically, it's true, once they have sold the weapons, they will be exempted from any wrong doing. It will be the responsibility of those who purchased the weapons to act responsibly and morally correct. But. My argument, as you will hear throughout, is this? Who then will be the one to be accountable for all this? Who then will be the voice of the voiceless? Who then will say enough is enough we can't watch when they kill young kids? Who will defend the children that are dying on a daily basis in war-torn areas? Who will say enough is enough they should be held accountable? If you were a kid, a kid that lost a leg, an arm or a kid that lost a parent, will you not want this to stop? This has gone for a long time, profits are prioritized than human life. I will show you today that these companies make billions in arms sale to third world countries, to war prone zones and to anyone if they have got the money. In their hay days, they have seen the war, they have seen fighting, we can't blame them. I say, we as the future generations we have never seen the war and we pray and hope that we will be the fortunate ones to never witness a war. It starts with us. Ladies and gentlemen, if you were that kid that was killed by a bomb, by a gun, by shrapnel, would you not want to know why? For decades, these tycoons have gone their way and did what is right to them but we are the future generations. We want a world where there is peace. Where my daughter will play with your daughter. Where my son will marry your daughter. Having said that, I am going to argue that some stereotype thinking has a major influence on the decision to continue to manufacture these weapons regardless of the consequences." A man, in an expensive suit, got up, and cleared his throat and walked in front of the court. He looked at everyone and walked to the balcony separating the people and him and held the balcony rails with both his hands. He looked at everyone and then stood upright. He pushed his sleek hair backward and looked at everyone and then at a man sitting in a chair in the far corner. "Today you have heard a lot of grumbling and okay I must admit, there are some truths in there but I want all of you to know this. Listen very carefully. Yes, the suit I am wearing might have been bought by money received from guns' sales. Yes, the car I drove today coming here might have been made with money from a weapons sale. Yes, the house I live in might have been bought by money from a jet fighter plane sale. Ladies and gentlemen this is like any other profession. A doctor buys a car, and the car kills a child would the doctor stop practicing? If a prescription medicine kills a child will the pharmacist cease to work because a kid died? Ladies and gentlemen, I want you to know that yes, my client sales weapons. Yes, there is a chance that the weapons might end up in the wrong hands but I want all of you to know this. My client took every reasonable step to make sure that the weapons were to be used in accordance to the agreed use. After that, my client's assumed responsibilities cease there and there. From the beginning of time there was war, it has been there and even after us it shall be there and likewise people will keep on dying. Don't get me wrong ladies and gentlemen we feel hurt by the loss but I want to stress out that my client took every reasonable step to ensure that the weapons will be used per the weapons charter and that they will not fall in the wrong hands. It's a pity children are dying, but this is a civil war and has nothing to do with my client." There was a real buzz of voices as everyone started talking to each other.

"Silence please, I will have silence in court," ordered the Judge, an old-looking man, with reading glasses and a sulking face. He looked unconcerned and barely made any movements as the two attorneys addressed the court. It was only after the noise made by the people that he seemed to have woken up from a deep sleep but for those who have known him for some time, they knew that Judge Shepperd was one of the honest and most experienced judges in the town. He never showed how he felt when it comes to court matters, but trust me, he was one of the most conscientious and attentive judges you will ever meet. This was the beginning of a trial, a first of its kind brought up by the families of the victims. The pain and hurt has forced the parents of the victims to come forward and against all odds and try to hold the mega tycoons accountable for their actions. For decades, no one had successfully brought a case before the court. Most of the cases never reached this stage. They were thrown out at first instance. Everyone wondered how this case had managed to do what most similar cases had failed to do. The weapons business was now a multi-billion-dollar venture with revenues more than $50 billion per year. No one was against this but recently the rise of deaths of children have raised much concerns among those affected. Over the years, weapons were bought by the rich oil states of the north. Countries who were more concerned with power and status than with the harming of young kids and women. Recently an appalling scene was apparent, and this has seen a rise in conflicts among the poorest of nations armed by these mega tycoons. For decades, this has gone unnoticed. Rallies after rallies but still no change. Judge Shepperd had vehemently opposed any moves against these mega tycoons in the past. This, some suggested that could have been personal too, after having lived a luxurious life himself, thanks to his friends in the weapons business. This was like any other job he argued. Very few people would point a finger until the last few years. No one really knew the reason behind the Judge's decision to allow this case for a hearing. Some say that these were the last kicks of a dying horse and he wanted to be remembered for something good. His friends, including the accused were adamant that the case was going to be thrown out. "The court is adjourned and will be resumed after lunch all rise." Instructed Judge Shepperd hammering the table with his gavel and going out of the court. Everyone stood up and after that they started going out as well. To the other side of the court, a couple remained seated. They looked anxious, and it seemed they just wanted to sit there and wait for the return of the Judge. They looked very impatient. They hugged each other. In the far corner, the man who was seated in the defendant box, rose at the sight of his attorney. The way they were dressed said it all, they were the richest of the rich. Everything from the clothes they wore and the way they talked and walked sung of riches and grandeur. They wore expensive aftershaves that everyone wanted to be close to them. Their hair glittered and gleamed. They spoke for a while and looked at the couple who remained seated.

"Maybe they are hungry. Maybe they don't have money, maybe we should buy them something to eat? We are sorry about all this, but what can we do? We offer them money but they refused. I am hungry I need to eat are we going or what?"

"Don't talk to them, let's go and have something to eat. OK?" Advised Pablo. A heavy built man with the cleanest shave you will ever see. He looked young with a chubby face. He wore what seemed to be an Italian or some French expensive suit. He wore pointed shoes that seemed to be longer than his feet. The two men strolled outside the court.

"I am sure that you are very hungry let's go outside even just for fresh air. One hour is a long time," pleaded Rex their attorney. Hesitantly the couple got up and walked out of the courtroom to the park bench outside.

"My son is dead, they think they can buy us as well. I would rather starve to death than to be mocked like that. He was only six-years-old. He had not seen the world to be taken away from me like that, not in such circumstances. Yet these monsters come to court smelling like money showing off, while my son is being eaten by worms, underneath. What happened to this world? Where are the days when people would run to defend you? Where are the days when strangers would invite you and make you feel one of them?" Terence was a middle-aged man whose son had been recently killed. He was engaged to Hannah. These two had been childhood sweethearts. Hannah had unintentionally got pregnant which was welcomed by both. They had recently engaged just before the tragic struck. This was a disturbing time for the couple. A lot was going on. Few weeks after burying their son they were in court. They wanted justice for their son. The company had opted for an out of the court settlement which was vehemently refused by the parents. This was not because the company feared to lose, no. This was out of sympathy for the loss of the parents as they put it. The couple had seen it as manslaughter and unimaginable negligence. One hour seemed like a few minutes as all stood up as the Judge entered the courtroom and toward his bench surrounded by bulletproof glass all round. Not only him was protected by the bullet proof glass. The defendant box had bulletproof glass too. This was a high-tension-filled case as at one point the father of one of the victims nearly crossed the bar trying to take the law into his own hands. There were extra security guards inside and even outside the court for the judges, defendants and the witness's safety. Judge Shepperd bangs the gavel. "Please rise. The court is now in session, the Honorable Judge Shepperd presiding, all be seated." Instructed the bailiff. Rex the attorney of the parent's victim, stood up and touched his suit jacket before walking in front of the people. He stood in the middle and looked at everyone in the court. He looked at the parents of the victims and then at the defendant. "Ladies and gentlemen, I want you to understand that because of the negligence of the defendant the parents lost their son. If the defendant had acted reasonably responsible and refused to sell the weapons to poor people with no money for food or to look after themselves then this tragic could have not happened. I therefore hold the defendant accountable for his actions. This failure to take reasonable steps to ensure that his weapons will not end up in the wrong hands amounts to manslaughter. They can't claim a lack of foresight as their defense, as they were expected to have that foresight to know that their weapons might end up in the wrong hands." A sudden buzz of voices flooded the court. Everyone, suddenly started talking in the court.

"Order! Order! Silence in court!"

Demanded the Judge.

Pablo the attorney of the defendant gave a quick arrogant smile and touched his suit. Swiftly the court doors opened wide. A group of journalists and photographers gate-crashed the court. The Judge repeatedly slammed the gavel calling for order and silence. The court's bailiff and ushers together with the security guards ran to the rescue and pushed everyone out. Rex after arguing his case before the Judge, looked at the parents of the deceased and after a while, he sat down. Quickly and energetically, Pablo got up and corrected the position of his trousers' belt before touching his suit jacket. He looked at Emmanuel who was seated in the defendant box. He walked toward him and looked at him. The two men shoot each other a quick glance. Pablo stood aside and looked at the jury and the Judge and all the people in the court.

"Ladies and gentlemen, we are not disputing that a young innocent life was lost, no. We are very distressed and pained as much as the victim's parents. We have done everything reasonable to us to ensure that the weapons were used in accordance to the weapons and Arms act. In fact, we went to the great lengths of offering any kind of help requested by the parents of the deceased, but help was denied. The question you should ask yourself is this. Did my client shoot this little poor kid? Some might argue that guns don't kill people, people kill people. Even in the harshest scenario, my client can't be held responsible to what happens after the sale has taken place. The Arms act is his bible. I am not saying that he did not take any reasonable steps to ensure that the guns were used in a correct manner, no. He went further to do a background check, and he looked at the history they have, as they have been doing business together for some time. All the facts point to a responsible and reasonable approach before and after the weapons sale. However, in circumstances beyond his control the kid ended up dead, even in this case my client had no part in any of what followed. Therefore, I want you to come to the same conclusion as me and see that my client's profession is like no other profession. This was an accident and my client had no foreseeable foresight that this will happen and pinning this on my client would be unfair. Thank you." Pablo remained standing for a while before going to sit down. Rex got up and walked toward the defendant and looked at him.

"Don't be deceived by the looks or the expensive clothes. Yes, we all admire the defendant. He is the symbol of the American dream but let us not forget that a young life has been abruptly ended. My question is this; who do you blame? Everyone says that they have done what they were supposed to do. Everyone is saying it's not their fault. So, I ask you, if you were the young kid that died, who do you blame? Maybe let me put it this way. This young boy probably didn't know what death is. Why? Because his parents never thought that he could be taken away from them in such circumstances. So, do we blame the parents? The defendant is saying that it was not his fault although he admitted the gun used and the rocket-propelled grenade was made by his company.

So, who do you blame? Everyone is saying it's the kid's fault, so it seems. Ladies and gentlemen throughout the court I am going to show you that the defendant although he refused to be accountable and responsible, he is very much accountable from the minute he thought about making the gun until the time he sold the gun and even after he had sold the guns. It is hard for us to apportion blame because history has refused to serve the truth preferring to give immunity and cover the rich and powerful with big pockets with acts that exempts them from being responsible and accountable. Acts that removed the assumed responsibilities."

"Objections, your honor, the counsel is misleading the jury by assuming facts not in evidence."

"Overruled!" Instructed the Judge.

Pablo sat down and watched Rex about to tear up Emmanuel. Everyone looked and watched attentively. A few journalists gate-crashed in. The usher looked at the Judge who in turn raised his hand. With everyone seated. Rex shot a quick glance at Emmanuel as if he was going to devour him with his eyes. Emmanuel looked at Pablo who slightly nodded his head as he sat comfortably in his seat.

"Ladies and gentlemen, I am going to show you a series of evidence that will prove that the defendant acted negligently and that failure to foresee the consequences not only is it gross negligence but amounts to manslaughter as well. I argue therefore that the defendant was indeed indirectly responsible for the death of the victim. I give you exhibit one."

Rex walked first to the Judge and then to the jury box and gave them a photo that showed a little boy.

"Objection. Best evidence rule. The counsel is

provided evidence not previously submitted. I ask the court's permission to approach the bench. Can we come forward your honor?" Requested Pablo.
"Counsel to my desk."
Directed the Judge.
The two attorneys approached the Judge's bench for a conference.
"Counsel, can you tell me what is going on?" Requested the Judge.
"This will come clear after the questions your honor."
"OK, you may proceed but be careful where you are going with this." Directed the Judge.
"How long have you worked for this company and in what role?" Asked the prosecuting attorney Rex.
"Objection, it is irrelevant your honor." Argued Pablo.
"Your honor. I want to establish assumed responsibilities and accountability. I also want to clarify the link to the role of the defendant in all this. May I?" asked Rex.
"Yes, you might proceed." Agreed the Judge. Emmanuel looked at Pablo who nodded his head slightly.
"So, what was your role with this company and how long have you worked for the company?"
"I have worked as the CEO for the past seven years." Replied Emmanuel.
"So, it is also true to say that you were the one responsible for approving most of the decisions and the signing of deals?"
"You can say that," replied Emmanuel.
"So, it was solely your decision to sell the weapons to these vulnerable poor countries?"
"Objection your honor. Counsel is assuming facts not

in evidence," argued Pablo.

"Counsel be careful, watch where you are going with this," instructed the Judge.

"I will rephrase your honor. So, if it was your duty to sell the weapons is it also not your duty to make sure that those buying your weapons will use them responsibly and to take every precaution to make sure that they don't end up in the wrong hands?"

"Objection, your honor, the counsel is provoking the witness."

"Overruled!" Orders the Judge.

"Let the defendant answer the question."

"My job is to make sure that the customer complies with the weapons charter but after that I have no control to whose hands the weapons end up into. Yes, it is my duty and I only sell weapons to people who use them as agreed."

"But is not true also that the same weapons end up in the wrong hands?"

"Objection your honor counsel is leading the defendant."

"Sustained, counsel can you rephrase your question," Commanded the Judge.

"You know that. These are serious accusations that can't be taken lightly. I want to establish that the minute the defendant decided to sell the weapons, there is also the assumed responsibilities to a society which he must consider. He should therefore take reasonable steps to ensure that they won't fall in the wrong hands." Rex stopped and looked at the Judge and then at the jury and then at the members of the public.

"Ladies and gentlemen of the jury, I am here to establish that he defendant ignored his assumed or implied duty to take every precaution to ensure the safety of the deceased. It is his duty and whenever in doubt, to not even sell the weapons."

Rex walked to the defendant and stood next to him. Everyone waited impatiently. The only noise that could be heard, was that from the corridor outside as they heard a woman coughing. "Is it not true that you chose profits instead of a duty of care to the victims?"

"Objection, your honor, counsel is assuming facts not in evidence."

"Overruled. I think this is fundamental to this case. Please answer the question." Instructed the Judge.

"It's not true!" Replied Emmanuel.

"So, who had the duty to ensure that no harm befall the victims?" Emmanuel did not answer the question. Rex paused and looked at the jury and the members of the public.

"Did you sell weapons to a one, Amorini?"

"Yes, I did." Replied Emmanuel.

"Did you not think that he might have been buying weapons to resell?" asked Rex.

"I followed the weapons charter and all the regulations. He checked-out. He assured me he was acting on behalf of his client a well-known customer."

"Was there a chance that profit might have been the main cause driving him to buy guns from you?" Asked Rex.

"That has nothing to do with the issue. Once he passed the vetting process, we have no influence in whatsoever happens after that." Everyone started taking in the court only to be silenced by the Judge. "Silence in court!"

Rex went to his desk and took out two photographs and gave one to the Judge and the other one to the members of the jury.

"Your honor and members of the jury. The defendant chose profits instead of a moral duty to the victims. In the exhibit two, the weapons sold by the defendant ended up in the wrong hands. Resulting in casualties. If the defendant is not responsible, then who is responsible? I ask you? If you were the victim who would you blame?" Rex looked at the jury and waited for the photo to pass around before he walked to his desk and sat down. Pablo got up and walked to the jury and took a long breath.

"We all feel sorry for what happened here. No one wants to see a young life ended like that. But ladies and gentlemen if we are to point fingers then society will stop to function as we know it. People die and children die too even in hospitals. Is it the defendant's duty to ensure that weapons don't get in the wrong hands? Yes, but how far can he go? He did whatever was reasonably right to ensure that the weapons don't end up in the wrong hands. He had immunity given to him by the law of this land through the Arms act. Assumed responsibilities ceased after the sale. In war times, children die but has the government ever been dragged to court? These things happen no matter how sad the story is, he can't be blamed for the death of this young life. No matter how harsh this might sound. He acted within the law." Pablo went and touched Emmanuel's shoulder before walking back to his desk. The court doors instantaneously opened. A young woman entered the court walking nervously. Rex's looked at her and smiled. Pablo looked at the young lady first, and then at Rex and soon after at the Judge. Rex quickly opened the envelope and looked inside. All eyes were fixed at him. He quickly went through the documents and smiled. He quickly got up and asked for permission to approach the Judge's bench. He approached the Judge's bench. He whispered something to the Judge. The Judge then instructed Pablo to approach the bench. The three of them had a conference. Pablo after the conference did not look very happy. He looked at Emmanuel with a strange face.

"Counsel you may proceed," commanded the Judge.

CHAPTER TWO

Somewhere in the suburbs, it's early in the morning. A smartly dressed man walked out of the house and into a car parked outside. He opened the back door and placed a suit jacket inside the car. He drove off heading to the city center. He received a phone call and answer the call using the car hands free system.
"Hello, Dominic speaking."
"Yes, Sir. I am afraid that the appointment has been rescheduled to later in the afternoon at two o'clock to be precise, you might as well take the morning off work."

"Are you sure, because the chairman wanted this to be done the first thing in the morning?" Asked Dominic.
"Yes, Sir, he is the one who asked me to call you," replied Evan.
"OK, I guess I have to take the morning off." A car continued until the next right turn. Dominic had

looked forward to this meeting, he had not even slept enough. He had five hours to himself that morning and so he decided to go to the city and back home. "Yes, sir how can I help you?" asked the shop assistant. A blond lady in her late thirties with piercings and a tattoo on her chest and neck. She had a nose piercing and was wearing glasses. Dominic looked at her for a while.

"Why would a beautiful girl go to such length for something that makes her look like that? I don't get it." Dominic asked himself as he was thinking aloud. He never seemed to understand all these new things. He was old fashioned I guess. He wanted everything to be as natural as it can be.

"Oh, yes, I need a packet of cigarettes, as well as this," requested Dominic handing her a bunch of flowers. He looked outside and saw a lady get charm, beauty and power. He felt an undeniable charm emanating from her. She slid her hair and with her hand pushed all the loose ends to the back. She looked in the shop and smiled before the driver on the other petrol pump gave a long glance. She smiled as another driver ogled her figure. She swaggered with style into the shop. Her taste of cars says it all, an extraordinarily eccentric woman, an automatic white BMW executive class. She entered the shop and everyone gave her a suggestive glance. Dominic grabbed his change and his flowers and nearly forgetting his cigarettes. As she passed him, he could smell the aura of perfume radiating from her, it was appetizing. Everything about her was just magic. Dominic remembered the first-time he met Audrey. It was magic, much more than this. She was a real charmer. He couldn't wait, the first-time he laid eyes on her he knew it straight away that she was the one. Dominic opened the car door and sat in his car for a while. Audrey had changed. He thought to himself. She was now a shadow of the woman she once was. She never paid any attention nowadays. Maybe it was because he was working long hours now. Life had changed for both since she gave birth to his son. They rarely spend time together lately, apart from doing chores like shopping and all the duties. He longed to reignite the magic again, to rekindle the romance that once was between them. At least today was the start. He could spend more time with her. He sighed and smiled before picking up the phone. He dialed his girlfriend, but she didn't pick up the phone. He set off heading back home. A car entered the driveway and Dominic got out and entered the house. As soon as he had entered the house, he heard his girlfriend shouting from the bedroom.

"Come up stairs, I can't wait, you seem early today." Shouted Audrey. Dominic for a second looked lost and confused. He closed the door behind him and carried the flowers upstairs. Confused. How did she knew it was him because as far as he was concerned, he was supposed to be at work, only if it wasn't for the phone call? A strange feeling struck him.

"No, it can't be," he thought to himself. He remembered trying to phone his girlfriend, and he sighed with relief. He gently slid the bedroom door open and stood at the door. He looked at his girlfriend and for some time he shot a lustful glance at her. For a while she did not look at him, she was busy running down her fingers all over her body half-naked and eyes closed. He looked at her and smiled, without saying anything. This is the woman he fell in love with. Full of surprises and one who knows the best points to press, at the right time.

"Flowers for you, my darling," announced Dominic entering the bedroom. Audrey jumped backward nearly banging her head on the headboard. She looked startled and quickly she grabbed the bedsheets and covered herself. She looked embarrassed or something. Dominic dropped the flowers on the bedroom floor. His heartbeat increased dramatically. Soon her phone rung, she quickly jumped toward the dressing table and answered her phone. She just replied no and quickly switched her phone off.

"Who was that!?" asked Dominic looking suspicious now.

"No one, wrong number," replied Audrey.

"Give me that phone, let me see. Why you switched your phone off." asked Dominic walking near where Audrey lay on the bed.

"No this is my phone. I do whatever I want with the phone. OK?" Suddenly the downstairs front door sounded as if it was opened.

"Are you expecting someone? Answer me?" Audrey closed her eyes and lay on the bed holding the phone tight in her hands. Dominic quickly rushed downstairs through the living room to the corridor and found the door slightly opened. Surely, he had closed the door behind him he ventured outside. He heard a noise made by the screeching of car tires outside and Dominic quickly went outside to look. He saw a car reversing out of the driveway, quickly he chased after it and jumped onto the bonnet. The driver looked backward and continued reversing the car out of the driveway. Dominic hanging on the bonnet tried to grab the man with his hand before the man swerved the car sending him flying on the ground. He fell and rolled to one side before quickly pulling his gun and getting up. He aimed as the car sped off but did not pull the trigger. He knelt for a while holding his knees getting his breath back. He got up and walked back to his house. He knelt and picked up a business card. He looked at it and stopped.

"Surely, I have seen this logo somewhere," he thought to himself. As soon as he entered the bedroom his four-year-old son came in.

"Daddy why is mummy crying?" Dominic picked up his son and took him back to his bedroom.

"Mummy wants to sleep. She is not feeling well. But everything is going to be OK." Dominic placed his son back to sleep and entered the bedroom. He placed his phone on the table and sat on the corner of the bed. Audrey was sobbing quietly.

"How long has this been going on?" asked Dominic.

"I was going to tell you," she sobbed for a while before blowing her nose.

"You are never here, for me, for us. Last time you were away for months. I can't have a life like that."

"I was at work, you know this is my job and we talked about this. Why bring this up now when I am about to leave."

"See that's what you always say. This time I am not going to wait for you. What about us? I told you to change the job. Choose, your job or me? You can't have both. You leave me this time I swear you will come back to an empty house." alleged Audrey.

"That can't give you the right to bring someone in our house when I am not here. Where would you go with my son? I can't let you take my son."

"You are never there for him so don't ask me where I will go with him. What kind of father are you? I swear if you go you will never see us again."

"If you take my son away from me I swear I will look for you everywhere. You better be joking."

"You think everything is a joke, wait this time you will believe me," suggested Audrey switching on her phone. As soon as the phone was on, the phone started ringing. Dominic out of anger stood up and grabbed the phone about to answer it himself when he got smacked across the face so hard that he saw stars flashing before his eyes. He kept holding the phone and was about to answer the phone when Audrey jumped off the bed to the dressing table and grabbed Dominic's phone. To Dominic everything appeared like in slow motion, she threw his phone against the wall. One piece landed in one corner, the other piece landed in another corner. He looked on the bedroom carpet and saw his phone in pieces and he looked up at Audrey who jumped at him. Before he knew it, she slapped him across the face once again. He threw the phone on the bed and slapped her once on her left cheek. He was about to slap her again when his son came out of his own bedroom. "Daddy I can't sleep. You are making noise." Dominic lowered his hand down and walked toward his son. He knelt and looked at him.

"Ah, very sorry you can't sleep. Daddy is going to work now look after mummy for me okay."

"OK daddy, I will, just don't make her cry OK?" Dominic did not answer but instead looked at his girlfriend who was talking on the phone.

"I am leaving you, I am taking my son, you never see us again."

"I am sorry babe stay. I will cancel this mission."
"Liar, I am tired of your games, I found someone who think about me, first. I am tired of being second best. I swear you will regret letting me go. I will tell my mum you beat me up. My dad is going to beat you up and make your life a living hell. OK you will see. You think I am joking." Everything looked unreal for Dominic. Just that morning he was expecting to spend quality time with his girlfriend and now this. He touched his head and sat down. Audrey entered the spare bedroom and dragged a small bag out. She quickly started packing.
"Darling don't go. I am going to work; can we talk when I get back from work? Forgive me, it all happened very fast."
"Today let us go, we can talk after when you return." Audrey's phone rung, and she picked up the phone and answered it.
"Oh, it's for you," advised Audrey giving Dominic her phone.
"Hello, Dominic speaking."
"Yes, Dominic it's the chairman, I tried reaching you on your phone but it's switched off. Listen we leave today. Get all your stuff and meet me outside my office." The line soon went dead.
"See, I told you, you, will never consider us first. I am leaving you." Somewhere far away, the night seemed peaceful with a cool breeze blowing around. A car is parked outside a big house and two men are seated in the car smoking and talking. The first man leaned forward and took a picture of a small boy on the dashboard and looked at it. He smiled and placed the picture back. A car came from the other end and the two men ducked down for a while. The other car

approached the big house and waited for the gates to open. The car entered the fortified building surrounded by a huge fence. The two men quickly wrote something down and waited in the car. The next day a car drove toward the big house and parked far away and waited. Hours later, a car came from the other side and stopped outside the big house waiting for the gates to open. The man in the car quickly wore balaclavas and one of the man dragged a long slim bag from the back seat and opened it.

"You have three minutes," informed one of the men. The other man frantically tried to put things together. The first man who happens to be the driver took out binoculars and looked at the big house before looking at his watch.

"Two minutes and counting."

He whispered. The front windscreen suddenly and slowly started retracting backward until it all disappeared. The gate to the house instantly opened and the car slowly entered the building. The man in the passenger seat aimed what looked like a rocket launcher at the car. As it entered the yard to the building the man with the launcher aimed skillfully and slowly moved his finger looking for the trigger and soon afterward they both heard a whistling sound. They closed their eyes as the missile left their car. When they opened them again, they saw a little boy running out through the gate as soon as the car had entered the building. A large blast sound is heard, and the car is lifted in the air as it burst into flames before thumping on the ground the two men ducked and shoot each other a long guilty glance. In the big city, it was business as usual. This was a busy and sensitive time for everyone. People had mixed feelings. People wanted to feel free, to live free without any fear of being attacked or surprised by a gruesome act. Most were calling for the government to go and flush-out potential future culprits from their hiding places abroad. The weapons manufacturing companies took this opportunity to market their weapons and show the full potential and use of their guns. Critics argued that the weapons manufacturing companies themselves had gone a step too far. Every day on the news they were incidents of young children dying on a daily basis. No one was prepared to take blame for that. One young man was determined to bring those responsible to justice. He knew that it was to start with him. No one will ever take the blame unless people's perception and stereotyping changed dramatically. This required enormous convinced and efforts. A woman knelt and picked up a newspaper from the shelf. A man was standing there reading the headlines.

"Who cares if they kill each other? Let them fight their own wars. We had ours why should we be bothered?" Declared the man.

"They are saying that we are supplying them with the weapons to fight." Replied the woman.

"Listen, even if we didn't supply the weapons they were still going to get the weapons from someone else. What we don't do there is always someone who can do that and provide the weapons to them."

"Some are arguing that if you look at their past civil wars. They never targeted women and children. Even if they died, it's not like nowadays. For years, they fought each other with knives and swords. They never maimed or killed any child. The weapons have made it easy to kill children. One bomb and ten children, dead. Now you see why the world is furious?"

"I guess you have a point but we sell responsibly only to people who use the weapons per the weapons charter."

"Ideally yes. But in reality, it is different. Most of the weapons end up in the deprived areas where they are used to kill innocent people especially children." The woman started walking toward the city center and entered a big building.

"Good afternoon Juliana what can I do for you?"

"I need the files I asked from you. It seemed this is never ending. They say money buys you freedom, and it seemed to be the case here. These weapons makers seemed to control everything and everyone. It's blood money if you ask me."

"Honestly, no one cares, blood money or not? This has become so rooted in the hearts and minds of the people that everyone now accepts and relates to this. Everything is now run with money from weapons sale. This is the new world, so, you should embrace it." Replied Jonathan.

"What surprised me is that the developed world is quadrupling weapons output, where are they planning to sell all these weapons. The strange thing is that in their own countries they have the strictest gun policies. One kid dies from a gun wound the whole country stands still. If hundred kids abroad die, no one gives a toss about this. Where is justice there? The rich get richer and makes more weapons yet putting in place the strictest rules. The poor with the limited money they have out of fear then buy weapons and let their kids die of hunger."

"What are you saying? Are you saying the rich

countries are contributing to this?"

"Exactly, look the richest countries interferes everywhere. Whenever brothers fight they are quick to send weapons. In the end, they kill each other. They are sending a wrong message. If they stop producing guns, then the poor world will have nothing to fear. Out of fear of being attacked, they buy the weapons. Are you telling me that these governments would rather buy guns when their children are starving. It's better to amour yourself than wait to be attacked. It is human nature."

"Honestly, I don't see how this is related," alleged Jonathan.

"Look Jonathan. It's a physiological game. The rich countries parade huge weapons to instill fear among the weak and the poor. Human instincts to survive kicks in. Instead of these governments buying food and the medicine they need, what do they buy? Weapons and defense system, they don't even need. Who is making all these? It is still these rich nations."

"You are just linking unrelated things here. Do you have anything against the rich and powerful?"

"Years ago, I was never concerned about this. But look at the rate at which young future generations are dying. Who will defend those kids? If you were that kid who would you like to see brought to justice?" Jonathan kept quiet for some time.

"This is how things are. Embrace this is the reality. The world you are trying to create does not exist."

"OK, but what I am saying is this; it has gone for too long unchecked. They keep making more weapons. Who is going to buy all these weapons? All the advanced countries have the capabilities of making the weapons. The third world countries don't have

the capabilities which is a blessing because they never needed these weapons and will never need them."
"It's a free market it's either you buy if you want or not. You sound like they are being forced to buy the weapons."
"No, Jonathan, I am just saying that they are scaring them into buying. Just a few weeks ago, one of the countries paraded a long-range missile and the next thing you know. One of the poor countries ran to buy a missile defense system. This is human nature. Human instincts to survive. When there is a threat you don't leave this to chance. That instinctively inherited from past generations." Julian walked out and crossed the road into the other building. She opened the door and entered the court. The court was very quiet, only sounds of people clearing their throats or coughing were heard. Things were getting exciting. The whole thing had turned a corner. The smile on Rex's face revealed it all. Surely, he was up to something. Pablo on the other hand looked perplexed and worried to some extent. Sweat started running down his forehead. Rex walked in front of the jury.
"This afternoon I am going to show the jury and the court that the defendant has no regard for the life of kids even his own." The whole court went berserk chatting to each other.
"Objection your honor, its inflammatory, and its intended to cause bias against my client."
"Counsel approach my bench."
"How is that relevant to what he is on trial for?" Asked the Judge.
"I want to establish credibility, a pattern of behavior, his own beliefs and whether they affect him in carrying out his job as well," explained Rex.

"Your honor I don't see how this is relevant, it's irrelevant this case is not about his person life. It's about weapons and his assumed obligations."

"I will allow it if you make this brief and to the point." Insisted the Judge.

"Do you have kids you yourself?" Rex asked the defendant Emmanuel.

"Yes, I have two girls."

"Is that all?" asked Rex.

There was a moment of silence. Emmanuel looked at Pablo. The Judge looked at both the men before ordering Emmanuel to answer the question.

"Just the two girls?" Rex walked to his desk and took two documents and gave one to the Judge and the other one to the jury.

"Exhibit 3, your honor and members of the jury in front of you are documents that say the defendant is not telling the truth. Why should we listen to everything he has said so far?"

"Objection, the counsel is intimidating my client can we have permission to approach the bench your honor?" Rex and Pablo approached the judges bench.

"Your, honor this can amount to new evidence and in such I request a recess to check with my client and I need time to look at the evidence first." Requested Pablo.

"Your honor, this is a background check of the defendant I can't say the counsel did not expect me to check his background and ask questions. In that light, I will argue that this can't be regarded as new material so adjourning the case will not be necessary."

"Objection overruled. Please continue," requested the Judge. Rex approached the defendant.

"How many children do you have?"

"Two beautiful girls and a boy," Noise broke out and a sudden buzz of voices flooded the court as everyone started murmuring to each other.

"Silence in court!" Demanded the bailiff as the Judge struck his desk with a gavel.

"Last time you said that two girls now you are saying two girls and a boy. If it wasn't for this evidence you were going to lie to the court yes or no?"

"I didn't think that was necessary."

Rex walked toward the jury and touched the balcony in front with both his hands. He stood up and paced up and down.

"Ladies and gentlemen of the jury. I am going to prove that the defendant not only pretended to forget about his son but that he doesn't care about his child at all. So why do we expect him to care for someone's else child? In that regard, I think whatever he is telling us should be treated with caution. The defendant as I am going to prove to you all, is that he does not understand what a duty of care is to his own kids let alone to these victims. How can we expect him to be responsible for his actions and safety of the whole society at large?"

"Objection, the counsel is assuming facts not in evidence," pleaded Pablo.

"Counsel can you support your accusations? Or I will hold you in contempt of the court?" Instructed the Judge.

"Give me time your honor." Requested Rex.

"Overruled."

"When is the last time you saw your son?" Emmanuel looked down before answering the question.

"When he was a little boy, about four years old." The noise broke out. Even the Judge just looked for a while before he slammed the gavel on the table. "Silence in court. Proceed."

"That's more than 30 years ago, are you telling me that you never even tried to look for him?"

"Don't lecture me about when and why I am not with my son. If it wasn't for that whore I could be with my son now. She run away, I never saw her again." The court started talking to each other again.

"Did you mean you scared her away? Did you beat her up?"

"Who are you to Judge me? You have no right to ask me these questions."

Angrily and agitated replied Emmanuel.

"Counsel rephrase your question."

Demanded the Judge.

"We can safely and reasonably say that it's true that you don't care about your son? Did you try to look for him?"

"I refuse to answer these questions."

"OK, can you tell the court your name?"

"Objection, irrelevant I don't see how this sits materially to the case beforehand," pleaded Pablo. "Let the defendant answer the question." Requested the Judge.

"I am Emmanuel Tronski." Rex quickly goes to his desk and took out two documents and gave one to the jury and the other to the Judge.

"Exhibit 4, this an affidavit showing that the defendant was formerly known by another name."

"Objection your honor. I declare the fruit of the poisonous tree. The evidence counsel is relying on was obtained illegally. Can we have permission to approach your honor?" Rex and Pablo approached the Judge's bench.

"These documents and this information can be obtained from the military public files," advised Rex. "Still, I need time to talk to my client this can be classed as new material." Pleaded Pablo.

"In the light of public truth, I would overrule the objection. This is a serious case. Young lives have been taken away, and it's for the public good to know exactly what is going on. You may proceed."

"Ladies and gentlemen of the jury exhibit 4 is a birth certificate of the defendant in military circles showing that he was formerly known as Dominic Tronski." The court bursts into noises as everyone started talking to each other. When Rex resumed talking they went silent again promptly.

"Not only did the defendant deceived the court about his children and his name there is more to it and in the end, you will find out that even you can't expect him to take the level of care required to safe guide the safety of the victims and the public at large." Pablo and Emmanuel shot each other a quick glance before Rex continues.

"Did you go on a mission when you were in the army. The days you were a young man.?"

"Yes." Replied Emmanuel.

"Did you kill someone when you were in the army?"

"Objection. Counsel is antagonizing my client. What happened in the army stays in the army, he was carrying out his duties,"

"Overruled. Counsel can you please stop disturbing the flow." Pablo looked as if he had already been defeated and he sat down like a dog putting its tail between its legs, in shame.

"Did you kill someone when you were in the army?"

"I guess so." Replied Emmanuel.

"Just answer yes or no. I repeat, did you kill someone when you were in the army?" Everyone looked at Emmanuel as he struggled to breathe.

"Yes!"

"Did you kill a young boy on one of your missions?" Reporters bursts inside and photographers and video cameraman started taking pictures. This time the usher looked at the Judge and all eyes were on the defendant. Pablo sunk his head down sitting in his chair.

"Did you kill someone else's son? Answer the question Damn it!"

Shouted Rex slapping the table walking toward the defendant. with a raised voice.

"Did you slaughter someone's son in cold blood? Did you intentionally and knowingly kill a child? A small boy. Someone's else kid? Answer me? Damn it! How did that make you feel? Have you forgotten? Do you want us to remind you?!" Rex furious, walked very fast to his desk and took three photos. He gave one to the Judge, the other to the jury and the other to the defendant's lawyer Pablo.

"Ladies and gentlemen of the jury and your honor, I present exhibit 5. Proof that the defendant not only slaughtered a kid in cold blood but lied about it under oath." Turning his attention to the defendant Rex grabbed the photo from Pablo and showed it Emmanuel.

"So, I ask you again. Did you pull the trigger that killed this young boy?" Emmanuel hesitated to answer. He picked up the photo and looked at it for a bit.

"Did you kill this little boy?"

"It was a mistake," replied Emmanuel.

"Answer yes or no. I repeat, did you kill this little boy?"

"Yes."

"Thank you. Ladies and gentlemen of the jury the defendant is a calculating man as you will see. He enjoyed killing people as a profession. Kids are no different. He is the CEO of a weapons company choosing profits to human rights and the life of these kids. Money comes first to him. He is not only violent to women. He killed a kid in cold blood too. He claimed it was a mistake but I am going to show you all that was planned. Surveillance went for days. A mistake is when something just happened. But the defendant for weeks put surveillance at a house targeting the owner. In the end, he cleaned out the whole family including this helpless little boy."

"Objection, the counsel is asking the jury to prejudge the evidence," pleaded Pablo.

"Sustained, counsel mind the road you are taking." Warned the Judge.

"After abandoning your own kid and killing someone's else, what guarantees do we have that you have been doing everything to ensure the safety of the victims? I find it hard to believe you care about the kids when you don't even think about yours. OK I am going to ask you a question. How many kids did you kill?"

"Objection, what is this, the counsel is antagonizing my client," pleaded Pablo?

"Your honor, I want to establish a pattern of behavior here. The world has trusted him to carry out his duties to the best of his capabilities. Thereby giving him greater responsibilities and if he can't manage his own affairs and his family and he has killed in the past, how do we expect him to meet his duties and obligations? This is open to me, to take this line of question." Explained Rex.

"Overruled."

"What happened on your last mission before you left the army?"

After a moment of silence Emmanuel cleared his throat.

"Most of the information is classified but I can say that I did not kill anyone. In fact, I disobeyed an order." The court bursts into noise.

"Order! Silence in court." Rex walked to his desk and took out three photos and gave them to all.

"Exhibit 6, the defendant in this case disobeyed an order to kill but the reasons behind his decision will soon be clear to all."

"Why did you disobey an order? Was this not want you joined the army for?"

"I was about to take the shot when an innocent kid immediately appeared," pleaded Emmanuel.

"So, let me get this straight. You are telling the court whole heartedly that you did not pull the trigger because there was a kid?"

"That is correct. I didn't pull the trigger because there was a kid among the target."

"So, you want us to believe that you disobeyed an order and risked being kicked out of the army because a kid appeared abruptly? Yes or no?"

"Yes."

Replied Emmanuel.

"Why did you kill the first kid?" Everyone looked at Emmanuel attentively as he took a long breath.

"Last minute after I fired the missile this kid ran out of the gate. We put surveillance for days we never saw a kid. Intelligence pointed to the same information. I regret that day. That's the main reason I never looked for my son. I took someone else's so I give mine away took." Some women at the back of the court were heard sobbing as Emmanuel spoke. It was so touching but Rex wasn't finished yet.

"Cleverly and touchingly said but still you went on to be the CEO in manufacturing weapons that are still killing kids. Pardon me, but I don't see any remorse and sympathy toward the kids. It contradicts the norm. You kill one, you learn from mistakes and never get involved, but you chose to make more weapons. You must see why I don't believe that you will do whatever it takes to protect the kids." Ladies and gentlemen of the jury. Today the defendant to me is still the same person he was years ago, a hungry gun mad person who will kill even kids. Putting someone like him as CEO will only make the world be hostile to the vulnerable. No one will be accountable for their actions. Rex turned back to the defendant.

"Did you try to kill your girlfriend?"

"No," replied Emmanuel.

"Did you try to kill your son?"

"What kind of question is that? No!"

Replied Emmanuel.

"Did she ever cheat on you?"

"I don't know."

"Just answer yes or no."

Emmanuel refused to answer.

"The day she left you did you not find her with another man?" Another loud buzz from the members of the court but soon after the court was dead silent.

"No."

"I repeat the day she left you did you not find her

with another man?"
"No. Yes, maybe. Look I don't know."
"Did you think that you didn't father your son?"
"What makes you say that he is my boy."
"Just answer yes or no," asked Rex.
"No."
"So, you are telling the jury that the boy is your son 100% sure?"
"Yes. 100% sure mine."
"Would you tolerate someone to hurt your son?"
"No way."
"In that case ladies and gentlemen, I want to present exhibit 7. The picture is of the defendant's son taken few days before he disappeared with his mum. The defendant was violent to his girlfriend."
"That's not true, I caught her trying to cheat on me. Apart from that moment I never laid my hands on her. Instead of apologizing she called him in front of me. She hits me a couple of times. I loved her. For nearly ten years we stayed together every day as a couple. That day my heart died when I saw another man waiting for her. If you loved a woman, the way I loved her, you would understand. Call me whatever you want but I loved her. I was out of the country and away with work all the time." Silence broke out for a while.
"OK if you confess that she was thinking of cheating on you that makes sense but still I believe there is more to it than meet the eye."
Rex walked to his desk and took only two photos one for the Judge and the other one for the jury. None for the defendant's lawyer Pablo.
"The last day you disobeyed the order would you say you acted rationally given the circumstances?" asked

Rex.

"Yes."

"If it wasn't for this boy you could have obeyed the order yes or no?"

"Yes."

Rex walked toward the Judge then in front of the jury. "Your honor, ladies and gentlemen of the jury can you please hold exhibit 6 and exhibit 7 together and look closely. It will make sense after I have finished talking to the defendant." Rex walked toward the defendant.

"You confessed in front of the jury that the boy in the photo is your son. You fathered this boy correct?"

"Yes, that is correct," answered Emmanuel.

"You confessed to the court that you did not look for your son after your girlfriend left you correct?"

"Correct."

"How long after the last day you saw your son did you go for your last mission the one you disobeyed the order."

"Two months after I last saw my son."

"What was your state of mind the last day of your mission? Did you think about your own son?"

"Yes, the last two months before that day. I was worried about my son. I thought about him all the time."

"So, is it possible that you did not shoot just because you related this boy to your son?"

"What?"

"Is it possible that this day you only disobeyed the order because your own son was taken away from you? Otherwise this was going to be another one of your slaughtering days. Yes or no?"

"Objection, inflammatory."

"Overruled I think it's relevant to the issue at hand." Explained the Judge.

"Members of the jury the defendant although he did not pull the trigger, this is only because he related to the boy at the scene at that specific time. I ask you to look at exhibit 6 and 7 at the same time." Rex walked to his desk and took a photo and gave it to the defendant's lawyer Pablo who sat up straight and looked at Emmanuel.

"Why did you not shoot this time?"

"There was a little boy among the target?"

"Is it true to say that you had missed your own son?"

"Yes."

"Is it true that this is the only reason why you did not shoot and why you disobeyed the order?"

"No."

"Is it true that you related to this boy? This particular boy only?"

"No."

"Is it true that this boy looked like your son and because of that that's the reason why you didn't take a shoot?

"No."

"Did the boy looked like your son? Have thought that it was your boy?"

"Maybe so but I did not kill that boy."

"Only because you related to the boy. If it was someone else's like in the first case, you could have slaughtered him too. Is that not correct?!"

"What? I don't know what you are talking about." Replied Emmanuel.

"Liar, you didn't kill the boy only because he looked like your son. Another kid you could have taken the shot."

"What! Don't call me a liar! I didn't shoot that boy."
"Only because you related to the boy. Otherwise you could have killed again." Rex walked to his desk and took two photos and gave one to the defendant. Emmanuel took the picture and looked at it. It was a picture of a blond boy. He squinted his eyes and looked closely.
"My boy, my son."
Rex waited for a while. He handed the other photo to the defendant, Emmanuel.
"What?"
He didn't even finish talking he looked at Rex, his attorney and the jury before looking at both the photos.
"See you can't even tell which one is your kid. In your mind is there a chance you might have not pulled the trigger only because the boy looked like your son." Emmanuel did not say anything he looked at the pictures.
"Did you not shoot only because you thought you will be shooting your own boy? Yes or No?"
"My son." hinted Emmanuel.
"I repeat did you disobey the order only because the boy looked like yours yes or no?" (Pauses)
"The only reason you did not pull the trigger is that you saw your boy. Yes or No?"
"The only reason you did slaughter that boy is that you felt like killing your own. Yes or No? Answer the question now? Emmanuel sobs for a while looking at the pictures.
"Yes. I felt like killing my own boy, my only son. I did not shoot. My boy, he is my boy."
"Ladies and gentlemen having heard all that my closing comment." Rex walked toward the front of

the court. He looked at everyone in the court and at the reporters and photographers at the back.

"This is a new chapter in the history of mankind. Gone are the days when people can kill kids and women and get away with it. Gone are the days when no one is hold accountable for their actions. We can't live in a world when we kill kids, irrespective whether it's your own flesh and blood or someone's else. We should bring these tycoons to justice if they act irresponsibly. They are destroying our generation, young generation. I sympathize with them for the fact that they have seen wars. They understand the need for weapons but that's about it. In our generations and generations to come. We want peace. You make thousands of guns today where are they going to end up? Who is going to suffer as you armor the poorest and scare them into giving you their only resources? Gone are the days when the rich manipulated the poor to fatten their pockets. Gone are the days when the rich preach of peace and love on their own soil and instill fear abroad and incite fighting among friends. We all should be accountable. The future is changing, there shall come a time when you will be put in front of a jury. The number of those with broken hearts, those who have lost someone is growing at an alarming rate I assure you that tomorrow things will be different. Your day to face the jury shall come to each one of you. Act responsibly and you have nothing to worry about. Act recklessly and I promise you that you will see the harsh side of the law. Money will not protect you that day. That law, that's protecting you today, ask yourself, will the law still be there tomorrow? Don't be complacent. Value lives." Pauses and continues.

"We are the future let not the old generation tell us how we will leave when they are all dead. It's up to us. Today I say put quotas on gun manufacturing. Improve other technologies that are beneficial. My recommendation to the court is that can these weapons making countries switch to finding and refining oil instead rather than making weapons and killing our future.

CHAPTER THREE

The anchor-woman on the news is talking about the court verdict.

"The weapons manufacturing company has been found guilty of manslaughter. For decades, they had recklessly killed and maimed innocent children while we look and watch. Today justice has caught up with them. The world is changing. Values are changing. Everyone should expect to be accountable for their actions. Today the CEO Emmanuel Dominic Tronski has been found guilty of manslaughter his sentencing will be next month. The Judge following recommendations by the prosecuting attorney has put a quota system. This will determine how many guns should be produced by the company as a way of phasing out gun production. After the agreed time frames gun production for exports will be illegal. To put it in another journalist's words. He reckoned that we should let them kill each other for a change. They should stop exporting guns to poor nations. The company had been given an option to invest in oil research, and development to keep their license. They can continue production in IT security, aircraft and other weapons. Its gun production that has been affected. Chantelle reporting for Touchladybirdlucky news." Seventeen years later.

"Seventeen years has passed since we embarked on a new project and ever since we have never looked back. This is the future, like the great speech of the attorney Rex, we must change and move with the times. I am very proud today to present out first prototype that will enable us to fulfill our goals moving forward. For the past seventeen years, we have made great strides," alleged the Vice President, a woman of substance. For the past years, she had been fundamental in the implementation of the new project. A huge door opened and inside is very beautifully decorated. It's a huge office room with two desks, the largest one being the one at the back. There is a display cabinet on the other side. The room looked luxurious with golden decorations. A woman entered the room and sat in the comfy sofa followed by a smartly dressed man. The woman is the Vice President.

"Yes, the reason I called you today is regarding our project. I need your approval so we can initiate the next stage Mr. President."

The President got up and walked toward the window. He looked outside for a while before looking at the Vice President.

"By approval, you mean you need more money? How much have you invested into this project Mrs. Vice President?"

"Mr. President, this is a big challenge, telling you how

much we spent will not do justice. Why not ask how this is going to revolutionize tomorrow?"

"Mrs. Vice President without sounding rude, I have been channeling public funds meant for other social programs to your project and seventeen years now and there is nothing to show for it. Main problem is that I am losing popularity. Everyday people ask about the missing funds and now you have the guts to ask me for more money?"

"We incurred unforeseeable costs and delays. I have used all my money on this project but I know with extra funding this will kick start this project. Sometime this week you can witness a miracle. A step toward evolution for mankind. We finally did it, although we are not sure if the mission will be a success or not, Mr. President."

"You are a great woman Mrs. Vice President, if you have achieved this surely that will be something. Myself I never thought that could be achieved. You promised that you will return all the money I contributed to your project, right?"

"With interest as agreed, fingers crossed sooner than thought, Mr. President."

"In that case then I have to approve the loan." It was night time, and it looked peaceful outside. The night was cooler with a breeze. After a long weekend, Elijah and Lily were driving home. Fatigue sat in and Elijah started dosing off. Lily was fast asleep. Elijah opened the window and lit a cigarette. He switched on the radio and drove for a while before abruptly gustily wind shook the car. That was terrifying that Lily woke up as well. It was just for a shot time but enough to have swerved the car.

"What was that? Were you sleeping?" asked Lily.

"Not sure what to make of this but I wasn't sleeping, maybe earlier on yes but it seemed a lorry or something overtook us and shook the car. I nearly lost control of the car." The car drove for some time before Lily screamed.

"Look out!!"

She shouted. The car came off the road and fell in a ditch. A small boy walked from the middle of the road? and looked inside the ditch and saw the wheels of the car still spinning. He stopped there for a while before he started walking in the road. Miles away in one of the towers an amber light is flashing, and the siren is sounding. Two men in the tower got up and walked toward the big screen.

"What seemed to be the problem?" Asked the Chief Security Officer.

"Unidentified object on the radar Sir." The main typed something on the keyboard.

"Alert security."

A van with security officers arrived outside a secured facility in the city. The men with guns started searching the yard. Another van arrived and troops got out and started running carrying guns. They searched the whole area too. It went for minutes before they heard a gunshot sound. Dean and Tanto were the first to arrive at the scene. One of their man lay in a pool of blood. He had been shot in the head. He had fired one shoot from his gun too it seemed.

"I need backup officer down north west of security tower over," declared Dean on the radio.

"He is dead. Let's spread out. You go that way, search the area. Meet here after 30 minutes." instructed Tanto leaving the scene. Tanto breathed heavily carrying a gun aiming at eye level. He searched the whole area. It was later that a sound from his radio sends him flying. It was Dean checking if he had seen anything.

"Nothing still checking," he replied. Just as soon as he had finished talking a boy appeared in front of him. The torch light on his shoulder distracted the boy. He stood there rubbing his eyes.

"Stand there lift your hands. Who are you with? What are you doing here? This is private land how did you get here."

Questioned Tanto. The boy looked at Tanto before he instantaneously opened his eyes shocked by the sudden voice on the radio. "Tanto, do you copy? Have you seen anything yet?"

"Stop! Stop! Or I will shoot!" Shouted Tanto chasing after the boy. He grabbed his radio and spoke with Dean.

"I need backup north west of the tower over." Dean ran as fast as he can toward where Tanto was. The boy ran as fast as he can as soon as he corners the building he clashed with Dean who fell to the ground. The boy just staggered and turned around and looked at Dean. A scream sound sends Tanto panicking. Surely it was Dean's voice, he ran as fast as he can. He came to the scene to find Dean on the ground touching his shoulder and bleeding. The boy stood there walking backward.

"What happened?"

"The boy, shot me," replied Dean. Tanto got up and aimed at the boy. The boy turned around about to run when Tanto opened fire. The boy fell to the ground. A siren was heard from far away Tanto stayed with Dean nursing his wound. In the Vice President's office, a knock on the door is heard and before the Vice President answered a man walked in wearing a military uniform. He walked very swift and looked very serious. "We have a problem Mrs. Vice President. Come with me." The Vice President followed the man through several offices until they have reached lifts.

"After you, madam."

The lifts took them underground. A man approached them and took the Vice President closer to the screen monitor.

"Yes, Mrs. Vice President, we have a problem. Our subject has been shot down right now he is being transported. From the satellite image, he is going north."

"So, what are you waiting for?"

"Please your authorization Mrs. Vice President," pleaded the Professor handing a small pad. The Vice President scribbled something before handing back the pad to the Professor.

"This is the part I like, now watch this."

They both looked attentively on the screen. This showed moving cars and lorries on the satellite map. After some minutes, one of the cars stopped. Suddenly a flashing beacon is seen on the screen before it disappeared. The Professor frantically entered some coordinates before a beeping sound becomes audible and consequently gradually increased.

"There seems to be a problem I think the subject is losing altitude," stated the Professor still typing coordinates.

"OK let me change camera to the subject's POV." After a while they saw an image of falling to the ground until they heard a huge thump and a line appeared across the screen.

"What just happened?" "Somehow it malfunctioned and lost power Mrs. Vice President."

"That's a billion-dollar project do you know where it crashed?"

"Yes, Mrs. Vice President. None of this should have happened. I think we are still having issues with vision related to different people and environments. We will need authorization as well to send our men to recover it."

"Granted, send them straight away. How did that happen I was going to introduce the project to the President this week?"

"I guess he must wait." A car drove to a secured building, and the person looked in the security camera before the gates opened. Dylan entered the building after arriving. He went to the underground lab. "Welcome Dylan, please come in," said Professor Duncan.

"Yes, I have been sent by the Vice President I need an update on the recovered subject."

"It turns out that the subject was shot. When we arrived, he had lost a lot of fluids? We are considering finding ways of amending the situation."

"So, when do you expect to resume?"

"Once we are sure then I will let the Vice President know for the meantime, our main goal is to finish the rest of the project. The President is on a state visit to the neighboring country on a state visit. On arriving he spoke to the President of that country.

"As you know seventeen years ago, we agreed as a nation to cut down on gun production. We have enough reserves to last us the next 20 years. On top of that we have extra guns we would like to trade with you in exchange with oil."

"Oil for guns. Who would accept that kind of deal nowadays? Guns are out of fashion. Oil is the new thing. Just last week people were talking about the oil war of future years. Human rights and all these campaigners have removed easy money from gun production."

"We did a short research, even with current standards I think you will benefit from extra gun stocks after all, your oil production has declined sharply over the years."

"Cost are so high that extraction is not viable. Our oil is the heaviest with API of less than 10'. The oil is not of market quality we must mix it with lighter oils still it's very expensive."

"That's when we come in Mr. President. We have qualified scientist who can look at making the oil of higher grade at a fraction of current costs. That will make it cheaper to transport as well." Later, in the news the anchor-woman is reporting the news about the oil deal.

"The President has arrived today from abroad after failing to secure an oil deal. Talks had been ongoing for some time until they stalled again last night. The pressure from other members of the oil industrial has again hindered progress. A decade or so ago, weapons and armor was the most lucrative industrial but oil seemed to be the likely cause of future world wars. Mira reporting for Touchladybirdlucky news." A bird flew in the sky before gliding down. An aerial view show the residential suburbs. On the ground a dog ran across the road and entered one of the yard. A car drove from down the road at the same time and entered the yard of a suburban house. Upstairs in one of the rooms a young boy looked outside from the window. Across the street, a girl looked outside the window and waved at the boy across the street. The man got into the house after parking the car. The man entered the house and into his study room. The boy gestured at the girl first before heading downstairs. He saw the study room door opened and peeped in. He saw his dad lifting one of the floor planks and took out a small box where he placed a small piece of paper and placed back the box. Soon after the boy entered the study room.

"Daddy you are back already what did you bring me?" Shouted the small boy. His name was Josiah.

"I brought you a motor bike it's in the lounge room. Go and check?" advised Samuel.

Josiah ran downstairs and Samuel heard his son celebrating and laughing. He smiled as he took his tie off. Years later Josiah is at the funeral. He looked around and saw his friends over the other side. Gabrielle held his hand tight when she noticed him looking around. He looked at her and for a moment forced a smile. It was the voice of the priest that caught his attention. He looked at his mum and saw her sobbing. After some time, he noticed a man standing across the cemetery. He was by himself and looked in their direction. He was there until his father was put to rest. After the funeral as he was about to get into the car he heard a voice behind him.

"Hello, I guess you are Josiah. I knew your father I am sorry about your father."

"Who are you? How did you know my father?"

"We worked together? I am Brian."

"Brian how come he never mentioned anything about you?"

"He talked about you all the time."

"I guess I must go. Been a very long week."

"I understand but your father was murdered it was not an accident."

"Who would murder him and what for? They insisted that it was an accident I don't see any reason to believe otherwise."

Brian took out a small piece of paper and gave it to Josiah and left. Josiah took the paper and folded it in his pocket and drove off. Far away a private plane landed on a field and three big cars approached the plane as it came to a halt. The door of the plane opened. A man wearing glasses got off the plane. Two other men started unloading cargo into the car from the plane.

"The first shipment two more later this month and the deal is done. The boss asked if you can pay in advance and you will get to get the cargo even earlier."

"No problem. Is everything for the first shipment there?" Asked Cole.

"Everything as ordered." The Vice President is in a limousine and she is talking on the phone. The Vice President's motorcade included, a motorbike in front then her limousine and an SUV then two more motorbikes at the back. Somewhere out of the city the motorcade entered a huge construction site. The Vice President viewed the construction site. Later she entered the office.

"Very grandeur project and this has been going on for the past seventeen years. Has this been completed yet?"

"This year, phase one of the project will be ready. Everything is nearly complete. We have problems of obtaining some raw materials needed. We will buy some soon, in fact we have ordered some from abroad."

"What else is needed before the project can commence?"

"Everything has been ordered and most of the stuff will be delivered this month."

The Vice resident later toured the site. The project was gigantic. The Vice President had a vision but for most this never made any sense. It was a waste of $billions. No one really knew why she had invested most of her money into something even banks refused to support. Only her knew. A lot was at stake. She had borrowed heavily in recent years after so many problems. On her way, back, the Vice President received a call asking her to watch the news.

"A young boy was spotted in the waters of the coastline. Locals have suggested that there have been several sightings of this boy in the water but after seeing him he then disappeared into coastal water. The locals have confirmed this was a legend of the lost boy that seemed to have come true. Today, the eye witness was so sure that he had seen the boy he called the coast guard and as we speak search is currently underway. I will bring you an update later. Christie reporting for Touchladybirdlucky news." The Vice President picked up the phone and dialed a number.

"Hello, it's me have you watched the news lately?"

"Not really been on vacation, Mrs. Vice President. What has happened?"

"Sort it out quickly."

Soon after she put the phone down. XVX was the leading weapons manufacturing company before the court ruling seventeen years ago, ever since it has seen its sales decline over the years. They have increased production in other sectors to make up for the lost gun production revenue, but operating expenses had remained high. All licenses for gun production had recently expired. This had seen the new CEO Mrs. Michelle open doors to innovative ideas. At one point, she had a meeting with the Vice President but it seemed nothing is known as the meeting was held under closed doors. Josiah father was an auditor and part of his job over the years was to audit privately owned companies to ensure they were adhering to the court ruling. The day Samuel died he was on his way to one of the company's place. As it was reported on the news, he had an accident in which his car crashed on a lamp post and the post caused a fatal wound. Weeks after Samuel died a car was parked outside his house. Two men got out and entered the house. The time Josiah came back he found the place vandalized. Clothes, papers, books and drawer cabinets were all over the floor. Josiah checked his small box he kept his stuff and took out a small note given to him by Brian. He opened the note, and it read XVX. He started researching about this company. He picked up the phone and arranged a meeting with Brian.

"Why XVX? Are you saying these people got my father killed? What do they want now, my father is dead?"

"Your father after I spoke to him he was adamant that he was going to do the auditing. The company had still paid him but had insisted that their own auditor do the job. The day he died he was going there. They alleged it was an accident but I don't believe them."

"Why would they kill him? They seemed like a clean company. I understand the Vice President does deals with them as well, so they must be clean."

"Did your father ever told you anything to you about this?"

"No. We rarely talked about his work. Why do you think he was murdered?"

"The day he died he phoned me and told me that someone was trying to kill him. He didn't sound scared or worried so I just ignored him. It was a shock to learn that he had died that day. XVX must be dirty somehow."

"Your father must have kept some of the documents, which they are still looking for."

"I think I know somewhere he might have left them."

When Josiah returned, he came back with a small box. Inside were shipment consignment notes.

"Let me see that." Brian looked at the receipts.

"It seemed nothing has changed over the years, in fact they are now shipping more abroad than they used to."

"Are you saying they are still making guns?"

A truck passed a heavily secured place and soon as the truck went past Josiah got out of the car and walked to the gate.

"I am an auditor I am here to carry out an audit."

"Take a seat someone will be with you soon."

Later the receptionist told Josiah that he had to book an appointment first. Josiah left the company.

CHAPTER FOUR

A ship is passing the coastline. Been very sunny when instantaneously the people in the ship noticed a small boy sat on one of the rocks in the middle of nowhere.

"Is that a small boy over there? How did he get here?"

"Surprisingly yes, that is definitely a boy."

The people in the boat started whistling and shouting. The boy stayed there for a while and when someone jumped into the water the boy escaped. Zack swam as fast as he can toward the place where the boy was before. He looked everywhere. It seemed the boy had disappeared. They looked everywhere around that place but the boy was gone. Zack jumped onto the rock the boy was seated. The place was hot, and they were oils of some kind. He looked around and saw some oil on top of the water. He looked around that area for a while before he went back to the boat.

"Strangely that boy disappeared. At one point, it felt like I was hallucinating."

"I am sure I saw the boy too. Maybe he is a merman," alleged Phil.

"I don't believe in mermaids or merman. That was a little boy I saw there."

"He must be with someone possible extracting oil. I saw some but, not much but just a few oil deposits where he was."

"In that case, he might have been with someone who is illegally extracting the oil." In the surrounding coastal area, a small boy walked in the forest near the coast. He knelt and looked at the small insects. He looked every, twisting and turning, intrigued. A snake appeared from nowhere and instinctively the boy jumped upward but the snake proceeds on its way. The boy then followed the snake for a while until it disappeared in a hole. The boy knelt and looked inside. He placed his hand inside. When he dragged his hand out the snake was biting his fingers. He looked at his hand and opened his eyes and mouth wide open with no other facial expression. He didn't scream as you would expect. He looked at the snake for a while and dropped it down. He knelt and saw the snake slithering away. The boy got up and walked toward the sea waters. He looked at the edges of the sea water and saw a death bird covered in crude oil. He picked it up and examined it. He looked down at his legs and saw crude oil in the water which slowly started getting absorbed into his body. The crude oil on the dead bird body slowly is sucked into his skin. He kept walking on the beach and all the crude oil that was in the water got absorbed into his skin. Haile, her husband Luke and their son Gregor have just won a vacation of a lifetime. Gregor looked very happy and surprised. They boarded a boat, and they traveled along the coastline. In the city center Professor Duncan is in the lab when the Vice President knocked and came.

"Yes, Professor what seemed to be the problem."

"We still have a problem with the grade of the oil Mrs. Vice President."

"I thought you declared that issues were resolved."

"Yes, but yesterday we received new data on one of our subjects. Somehow the subject is absorbing oil through the skin. This oil is not treated. Viscosity is dense therefore it's slowing it done. It hasn't moved since the last time I checked."

"The good news is that after 17 years, I think we have reached the crucial point. Only that we have not anticipated this coming. Or should I say this was a quick way of locating the oil? Don't it forget it was 17 years ago, when it all started,"

"So, what are you saying Professor?" The Professor, took off his reading glasses and stretched his hand. "Congratulations Mrs. Vice President, 17 years of challenging work has paid off. In all locations, the subjects are done." The Professor quickly switched the satellite monitor screen and showed it to the Vice President. The Vice President looked at the screen in disbelief. There were red beacon flashing points on several points on the world map.

"Are you sure Professor all areas that can't be right, at the same time?"

"It's correct Mrs. Vice President. Initially, we calibrated the subjects in such a way that their speeds where different. These were per several factors like depth and type of the rock its hardness and composition but completion time frames where the same." The Vice President smiled for a while. She paced up and down.

"Yes, Professor so can we commence phase two."

"Definitely without delay." In one of the surrounding country there are riots in the city. Cars are being burnt down and the shops and building are all being looted. The country is in chaos. Branden walked into a hotel and sat on the table. He looked at the television and asked the hotel staff to increase the volume.

"In an unexpected turn of events the government of the neighboring country has called an emergence day. The country is in chaos. The people have been rioting for days now. They are calling for the resignation of the President of that country, this is in line with the recent increases in food prices and shortages of basic commodities. It is reported that the President had turned down a lot of offers for oil deals hoping to trade when oil prices had gone up. Surely the people it seemed can't wait that long, they want him out."

The President was in his office when the phone rang.

"Yes, Mr. President it's Branden, I think it's time to negotiate that deal. I understand he has been making offers."

"I must talk to the Vice President first, I think she will be excited to hear this she has been pushing this for a while now."

The Vice President is in her limousine when her phone rang.

"Mrs. Vice President I have got very good news for you, we have been offered the deal even better now."

"No, Mr. President refuse the deal."

"What? What did you say Mrs. Vice President?""

"Abort, not the appropriate time for making deals."

"I can't believe you said that. All these years you were pushing harder for this deal so what happened?"

"Morally I can't accept the deal now. It will be getting the oil at the expense of the people."

"They are rioting they need food, why would they care about the oil they can't extract the oil themselves."

"Mr. President. I have a bad feeling about this. Can we talk when I arrive I am on my way there." Later the Vice President and the President are in the office talking.

"Yes, Mr. President, ignore this deal for now let the riots cool down then negotiate. In the meantime, I need more money for the project we started years ago,"

"More money. Few weeks ago, I approved the funds. Now you want more money? I don't think it's a good idea. If someone is to find out about this, we are both finished. My plan was to make the oil deal now. If someone asks about the money what should I say. That Branden, he is on my back all the time."

"You are the President you can always think of something to say."

"Last time you promised to show me the progress, but you never invited me. I am the President should I not know everything that goes on around here?"

"You should know that this is my private project so I have sole control."

"But most of the money is government money Mrs. Vice President,"

"Borrowed, loans which I will repay back Mr. President."

"Only this time I am asking you for your help. Support me. Oil is the new future all these weapons, I don't see it, really."

Months later the night was dark with no moon

and very cold. In areas around the show line the waves ebbed the shoreline sands. Kai had just arrived on the shoreline. He dragged his boat off the waters and set up a fire. He got his whiskey out and after grilling his fish he, had his meal. After some time, he started dosing off. Sometime at night he heard noises as if something was jumping in and out of the water. He got up and climbed the step on his boat and looked outside. He saw what appeared to be a small boy jumping into the water. Somewhere, far away Elliot and Declan are in the watch tower when a beeping sound becomes increasingly audible.

"What seems to be the problem?"

"I don't know Sir some kind of malfunctioning on the detectors part. I am seeing unidentified objects that quickly vanish over the sea waters. It looks like this has been happening for quite a while now."

"I think to be safe, can you send someone to check it out get the coordinates?" Later a patrol boat flashed the lights checking for anything suspicious.

"This is the coast guard please come out of the boat with your hands up." Kai got out of his boat and spoke to the coast guard.

"Have you seen anything suspicious?"

"Not really apart from a small boy I thought I saw earlier on but I was drinking so I can't be sure." Replied Kai. The Vice President was in her office with the Professor watching the news.

"A plane has been diverted back to the airport after a passenger told staff that she had seen a little boy in mid-air outside on the wing of the plane. The pilot as a precaution landed back at the airport. This is the first-time we have heard something like this. The plane was searched after landing and appeals have been made on the ground but it seems no one else saw this boy. Gianna reporting for Touchladybirdlucky news."

"So, Professor what are the current problems and how do we tackle this issue?"

"Mrs. Vice President there are a lot of issues. This has never been done before it is a learning experience. The main issue is that the oil is very heavy. This will slow the process and will be expensive in the long run. Our plan is to do it simultaneously. We get the heavy oil first and at the same time we get the lighter oil as well. We mix both as we go, the grade we will get after will be much easier to refine and process."

"Risks."

"Too many journeys all over, big risks are sightings and of being caught."

In the suburbs in one of the cities a young woman by the name of Rose, late thirties is outside one of the houses. She waited for a while before breaking into the house.

"Haile! Luke! Gregor!" Later that evening a police car parked outside the house. The house looked like it has been abandoned for some weeks now.

"Can you think of somewhere else they might

have gone, friends, relatives or for a vacation?" Asked the Policeman.

"Honestly, I don't know. I checked everywhere I can't find them. They don't normally go on vacation this time of the year. I think it's okay to file a missing person, report." One sunny day a small boy walked on the coast shoreline. He stopped and quickly reacted to the sight of the crude oil in the water. Quickly somehow the crude oil is absorbed through his skin into his system. After sometime he felt heavy and looked bloated. He sat down before sleeping but with eyes wide awake. Later that day a body of another small boy washed up to the shoreline. The first boy woke up and looked at the other boy's body that has just washed up to where he was. The body of the other boy somehow is washed up to exactly where the other boy is sleeping bloated and unable to move. The bloated boy lifted his hand and grabbed the body of the dead boy. At night water evaporated around the bloated boy's body. In the morning, the once bloated boy when he woke up, he was okay. He looked next to him and saw a lifeless boy next to him. Somehow the boy's body had shrunk and oils from the dead boy had been absorbed into the once bloated boy. He looked at him and shook him trying to wake him up when he didn't get up the other boy stayed with him the entire day. After some time, the water reached where he was and with it came some crude oils too. Soon after he found himself bloated again and unable to move. He looked around, it seemed another night bloated again at the same place. Some months later, at a ceremony, the Vice President was officially opening the new reservoir plant. A large crowd had gathered outside. There were reporters and news channels crews.

"Ladies and gentlemen, we have worked very hard in the past decades to make this nation a great nation. We face new challenges today many had voiced for a responsible government and we have done our best to achieve that. Today I will officially open the water reservoir that will help provide the much need energy in the future."

"Mrs. Vice President, was it not easy and cost -effective if we had just signed an oil deal?" asked one of the reporters. The Vice President paused and looked at the President who looked away for a while.

"Why we stopped gun manufacturing even when we were making a lot of money out of it? Anyone?" She looked at everyone in the crowd but no one bothered to answer her.

"For the same reasons. This oil is tainted with the blood of the local people. It was a great deal I must admit, but this project is a project to be proud of. The project is ours forever. We can be proud and call our nation a great nation without being accused of anything. When the time was perfect, the President of that nation refused to make a deal. This day and age, I personally think it's not a good idea. Maybe tomorrow things might change."

"Where would you get the water to run the turbines? Isn't that another cost as well?"

"Yes, the water. We are planning to build a water pipeline that goes all the way to the sea. Just imagine this project took us more than seventeen years but let all you know this is the future. A responsible government and a rich nation. Thank you." Everyone gave a round of applause and praised the Vice President before the President took over. Weeks after the disappearance of Rose's sister and her family, Rose moved in the house for some time. Her boyfriend Ezra moved in with her to help her while the search for Haile went on. One day they were watching the television after dinner when they heard a large noise on the roof. Ezra ran out to find out what was happening.

"Hello who is that? Gregor! Haile! Luke! Anyone?"

Rose followed outside and stood next to Ezra. They looked around but did not find anyone. They entered back in the house. They watched the movie and later went to bed. It was later when they woke up in the middle of the night when they heard the door being opened. They rushed downstairs and found Gregor laying down on the kitchen floor with oil on the floor slowly being absorbed by his body.

"Oh, my God! It's Gregor!" Shouted Rose. They

carried him upstairs to his bedroom and put him on the bed. Soon after he started shaking and his body temperature began to rise.

"Something is wrong his temperature is way high maybe we should call the ambulance."

"We need answer fast why not put him back in the kitchen maybe that oil on the floor was to keep him cool?"

Suggested Rose. The couple ran downstairs carrying Gregor.

"Honestly, I think he is too heavy for his size. Damn I feel like I have been carrying a huge person. My back."

"Get more oil quickly." Shouted Rose.

"Gregor, can you hear me? Where is daddy and mum? Gregor where did you come from?" Gregor did not reply but kept shaking, it took more oil before he stabilized.

"Is that natural? Where is all that oil going? But somehow his temperature is getting low and the shaking just stopped." After a while he opened his eyes and looked at the couple. He stretched his hand and touched Rose.

"He seems OK, but he is not talking. Maybe we should take him to the hospital. He could be in shock."

"I think he seems alright can we wait until in the morning let's see how he will be then."

"Let's take him in the bathroom in case he will start heating up. Bring the oil we can try water as well." They carried Gregor in the bathroom. They opened the water and as soon as he saw the water he got up and entered the tub. Ezra powered oil and for a long-time Gregor simulated swimming dipping his head and resurfacing. The pair went to sleep. Somewhere in the city the Professor woke up in the middle of the night. The siren and a beeping sound went off. He looked at the screen. Quickly in pajamas he telephoned the Vice President and left the lab. Later that night the Professor entered the Vice President's residence.

"What is wrong Professor, it's after midnight?"

"Mrs. Vice President this can't wait. We have a security situation. I can't understand what happened. Only probable reason is that the subject has been kidnapped or captured of some sort."

"Professor how is that possible you confessed they are not friendly to humans. They will do anything to self-preserve. So, what is the problem?"

"That's what I thought until this morning. Certainly, this one is way far away from the target area."

"What could have happened? Any chance it bloated again?"

"Mrs. Vice President, highly, unlikely. If it bloats, it doesn't move or fly. If approached by humans, the rules are to kill and escape."

The subject's current position is in the middle of an urban area. Any publicity will be detrimental to the project. You must authorize retrieval and cleaning up, promptly.

"And if something goes wrong?"

"Mrs. Vice President I can't guarantee anything, we haven't collected even a tenth of the target volume. All the billions will be to waste. We are running out of time." Gregor walked in the park and came to a big screen television in the city center. An anchor-man was reading the news.

"A couple had been found dead this morning. Somehow it seemed that they have been shot dead. Earlier reports suggest that the deceased's sister and her family disappeared. It is not known what happened but I will give you an update later this morning." Richie reporting for Touchladybirdlucky news.

"Mummy there is a boy in the kitchen! Mummy!" Shouted Paige. Lucy and her other daughter Molly came downstairs running.

"It's Gregor.", shouted Molly.

"What's with the oil mummy?"

Gregor opened his eyes and looked at all three before focusing attention on Molly with no expression at all.

"Gregor what is wrong? When did you come back? We thought you were dead." Gregor got up and looked upstairs. He started walking upstairs and into the bathroom. He opened the water into the bath tub and entered the tub. In the control tower three men and a woman are manning the tower when the system started beeping.

"Unidentified object has been detected."

The emergency lights started flashing, and a siren went off. Silas quickly picked up the phone. "Unidentified plane please identify yourself. I repeat please identify yourself. You are entering private airspace. You will be shot down if you proceed." Jet fighters were scrambled. They headed toward the unidentified plane. Subsequently something traveling at a very fast speed passed just above them.

"Wow, what was that?"

Shouted the jet pilot in the pa system of the plane. Soon after the object disappeared from the radar. At a private ceremony, somewhere in the city the Professor was with the Vice President unveiling the new models.

"I would like to take this opportunity to thank the Vice President. We are grateful to her unwavering determination and sheer power, without her today, mankind would not have witnessed something as miraculous as this. Ladies and gentlemen, I would like to present to you the new models," Revealed the Professor. Everyone was excited to see the new models. Everyone was delighted, and they applauded the Professor before the Vice President took center stage. "Thank you all for coming. In this new world, to survive you must go beyond the norm. This is proof that we are taking tomorrow seriously. We are building tomorrow, today. Thank you." One of the shareholders wasn't satisfied that the targets were going to be achieved within the given time frame.

"Given the current circumstances that some of the subjects had been shot down over private space what guarantee is there that such incidents won't occur again?

"In the first phase the main goal was with finding the perfect points for extraction. The first generation of these subjects are primarily for research, for drilling and laying the foundation for the phase we are entering now. Mind you these were made more than seventeen years ago; the new model is fast and cannot be easily cornered. This model is sophisticated. Can't be detected on the radar either. Above all this they can talk basic language and we can communicate with them directly from here." For the first-time the shareholders and potential investor were introduced to the new subjects.

"Hello, good to see you. I am TK."

Announced the robot. "Yes still, most of the oil is very heavy to carry. How are these robots going to manage that? How many trips they must make and what time frames are we looking at here?"

"True, oil is heavy to carry but over the years we have developed chemicals that makes the oil lighter without losing the value. The robots themselves process the oil before transporting it. Talking of numbers and time frames, like I said this is the future. Depending on the number of robots we will send I think the question you should have asked is, how fast are they?" Everyone started talking to each other.

"Ladies and gentlemen, shall we?" Requested the Professor pointing outside. A large buzzing noise of voices is heard as the investors and the Vice President walked outside. In the grounds of the property they stood drinking champagne and wine. After a short while a small plane hovered in front of them.

"Sneakiness, very fast and above all a sophisticated negotiating and processing subject, a human like robot."

The plane instantaneously landed, and a boy stood before them.

"We meet again, ladies and gentlemen," proclaimed the young boy robot. The Vice President and everyone there were perplexed and very thankful for such a wonderful technological advancement.

"Mrs. Vice President and ladies and gentlemen, I present TK the future, fast I mean fastest that any manned plane. Slick, surreptitiousness and a powerful processor."

"Yes Professor, tell me what is the carrying capacity?" Questioned the Vice President.

"We have developed a new way of transporting the oil. TK can process the oil as soon it is drained into his system. The problem we had in the first instances was that, after running out of oil, TK, ended up using all the oil himself."

"Naughty boy!" Yelled one of the investors. The

all started laughing.

"It's a fact, TK requires a great deal of oil too but we have harmonized everything and increased carrying capacity. Tubes build inside him are separated from his own system. This has enabled him to compress, heat the oil and mix it with advanced chemicals to reduce its weight. With more of these boys by the end of the year we will have collected a quarter of the world's oils." Everyone applauded and clapped hands. TK instantly jumped into the air and transformed himself into a small plane before he disappeared. Brian and Josiah were in the car somewhere in the city.

"I have an idea. All the receipts your father kept had been delivered to the same location, right.?"

"Right."

"I think if something illegal is still going on. The deliveries won't stop. Therefore, we should go abroad."

"I never thought it that way, I think that's the best way. I can't get access here, few days ago, I was refused entry." Weeks later Brian and Josiah are abroad in a hotel.

"Word in the town is that the delivery is on either Thursday or Sunday."

One early night Brian and Josiah left the hotel in a hired car. They parked near the air field landing site and waited. The first night there was no landing. The second time was on a Sunday after nearly two hours of waiting a private jet landed.

Shortly after three SUVs arrived and six men got out of the cars. Brian and Josiah from a distance took pictures of everything that happened that day. After the delivery, Brian and Josiah followed the cars. This took them to a remote villa out of the city. They parked outside a distance away and waited. After hours, the SUVs left.

"Do you think the cases are left in the villa or maybe they have gone by the SUVs?"

"I think they are left in the villa."

"Shall we?"

Brian and Josiah went to the villa. They jumped the wall and entered inside. They went to one of the windows and looked inside through the window. They saw a half-naked woman resting on the couch. Brian pointed to the other window and the pair sneakily walked to the other window. They took turns to watch what was going on inside. A man was there looking at the boxes that had just arrived. They had received guns. The man inside was carrying one in his hands looking at it. He looked to the window and aims the gun. Instantly Josiah ducked down.

"I thought he had seen me."

"Highly unlikely. Inside this time of the night you can only see your own reflection if you were inside. Let me look and see."

Brian looked inside. Another man walked into this room and he spoke to the man holding the gun. He placed the gun down and left the room. Brian looked up and saw the window open. He could easily enter through the window.

"I am going in. Help me get in." Hesitantly Josiah looked at Brian.

"Are you sure about this? I think it's dangerous." "Don't waste time, we came all the way here, without a sample it will be hard to prove. Help me get in quickly." Brian jumped to the top window rail and entered the villa. He had never been this afraid before. He crawled to the guns and looked at the labels. He grabbed one and crawled back to the window. He gave the gun to Josiah. He jumped onto the window rail and started getting out through the window. Only one of his legs was still inside before he let out the loudest scream Josiah had ever heard. Josiah instinctively got up and looked inside the villa. A large black dog was biting Brian's leg. Intuitively Josiah pointed the gun at the dog and as the dog jumped backward, he pulled Brian out.

"Let's go! Get up! Get up! Brian let's go!" Shouted Josiah helping Brian up. Josiah threw the gun on the other side of the wall. He pushed Brian over the wall and he looked backward and saw the dog about to make its way out of the window. He quickly ran toward the window and closed the window before he heard the door being opened. For a split second, he froze. The barking of the dog startled him. He ran to the wall and jumped over. He saw Brian limping toward the woods where they had parked their car. He looked backward again and saw a man aiming at him, somehow, he tripped and fell to the ground. Knowing that he wasn't hit he looked back and saw the man running toward him. He got up and quickly ran for his life. Brian started the car but entered the passenger seat. Josiah looked backward and saw now two, oh three men running after him. He quickly jumped into the car and reversed as fast as he can. The three-main stopped, and all took aim as he reversed. He swerved before seeing the windscreen shattered with bullets. He turned and drove the car at first as he kept checking in the rear-view mirror and the side mirror. After a few seconds the car swerved in the road before the tires came to a screeching halt.

"Brian! Oh no!"

Frantically he tried to stop the bleeding but Brian was dying, shot in the chest. Quickly he started the car and drove as fast as he can.

"Boss. Who are they?"

Inquired Enoch.

"Petty thieves I guess. Stole my gun."

Josiah looked backward and saw SUVs coming his way. Fear crippled him. He drove as fast as he can. He looked at Brian but he had died but still holding the gun in his hand. The pursuit was on. The car meandered from left to right following the road pattern. Constantly looking back at the SUVs. He ducked at the sound of the gunshot sound and the car swerved nearly colliding with oncoming traffic. He reached for the gun on

Brian's dead body and juggled between checking if the gun had bullets and driving.

"Damn!"

The gun had no bullets. He stepped on gas and drove as fast as he can, checking in the rear-view mirror repetitively. He knew it the SUVs will soon catch up with him. The road ahead was a junction. He held firmly the steering wheel. He looked on his right and saw an articulated lorry coming from the right side. He looked in the rear-view mirror and saw the SUVs covering the gap. He held the steering strong. He passed the junction in full speed nearly getting bumped by the heavy lorry and sending another car crashing into the lamp post. The lorry stopped just a few feet from his car. As soon as he had crossed, the lorry continued afterward thereby blocking the road for a while. Josiah covered a distance before one of the SUVs approached behind him spreading bullets everywhere. After a while the car bumped the side of his car and send him off the road. He soon finds his way back into the road. He looked to his left and saw a train going parallel and the same way as him. He looked ahead and saw a crossing point. He looked in the rear-view mirror before stepping on the gas pedal. He increased speed until the car started rattling, shaking, and vibrating. He looked at the train and instantaneously the train driver sounded the horn. Josiah proceed. The gate had already started lowering when he promptly past narrowly missed by the train. The SUV following him instantly screeched its tires to a halt. By the time the train had crossed he had been a long time gone. He left the car at the airport and boarded the plane heading back home with a concealed weapon. The phone rung, and he picked up the phone. "Watch the latest news," advised a man's voice before the line went dead. "In a surprisingly turn of events the weapons making company has had their license revoked. It apparently came to light that over the past years despite court orders they were still making guns for exports and selling these abroad. Jessica reporting for Touchladybirdlucky news." A reporter ran to a limousine that had just arrived and blocked the doors before a security man came and pushed them away. The door opened and the Vice President came out.

"Mrs. Vice President what do you say about the latest development? Do you think that this has been going on for years behind your back? Are there still other companies out there still illegally making these guns for export?" Asked one of the reporters. "We took a stiff stance and fined the weapons manufacturing company just to show how we are serious about this. Their license has been revoked as well. We have set up a task force that will look at this into more detail." Later that day the Vice President was talking to the President.

"Yes, another way of raising funds I guess."

"You can say that. The future is bright but to get there we must gather the resources needed today."
"Will people not say that you have turned a blind eye so that it will be easy to collect the fines Mrs. Vice President?"
"Whatever works they are not bothered, over the years they have made money they can easily pay the fines." "That brings me to the next question. Your project how far has it gone? Will I expect the loan repayments anytime sooner?" The Vice President smiled and walked away for a while. She turned around.
"Probably this year you might get all your money back? Fingers crossed."
"Really? That would be something. Why I don't get a full update on this project?"
"You are like a loan lender or a bank and that's about it. If you want to know more, then you invest more but you pushed idea aside. I have invested all my own money, I will return all the money I borrowed so I don't see why you should know every detail. In fact, this is for your own protection. Distance yourself if anything goes wrong you know your hands are clean Mr. President."
"OK, well said Mrs. Vice President."
A man walked very quickly and entered the Vice President's building. Up the lifts and into her office.
"Mrs. Vice President we have a situation."

Somewhere far along the coastline a boat is parked near the shoreline. The man is carrying a bucket like container collecting oil that is in the water. He looked around and swarm to the edge of the shoreline. He saw dead wild life and placed these in the plastic bags he was carrying. He looked scared and frightened by something. He edged forward and saw a skeleton in the shallow waters. He scanned around and saw another skeleton. He swam back to his boat and placed his samples in the boat. He stopped and observed around. He saw what looked like a human being from far away. He ran downstairs and brought back binoculars. He looked and saw a boy jumping into the water. He looked for a while checking for the boy. He moved back to the position he had seen the boy jump into the water. The boy had vanished. He looked at his watch. He quickly started his boat and drove toward the place. He looked around everywhere but did not find out anything instead he noticed that place had more oil deposits. Later that day the man carried an oxygen tank dressed in his diving suite and jumped into the water. After searching he heard a plane and saw a sudden movement. He heard a noise as if something left the water at great speed. He quickly swam to the surface and looked everywhere. There was nothing. He went back in the water. Further down on the same coast a patrolling coast guard is heading toward the man. Stan and Rodriguez are in the patrolling boat. "I have seen a boat, look over there," revealed Stan pointing ahead of him. Rodriguez took out his gun and when the boat arrived Stan jumped into the boat and stealthily searched the boat. He came out and pointed in the water. Terence was under the water when he saw a shadow above the water. Another boat had just arrived. He started swimming up. He was about to resurface when shots were fired into the water. Panic and shock sends him further down. He looked at his oxygen meter. His oxygen was running out. He swam deep further before he started seeing oil deposits. That made sense the boy was after oil. He went further down and saw a hole in the ground. The place looked dark. He felt scared for a while. He crawled inside the hole his heart beating fast. Suddenly he heard a large noise and something hit him in the face very hard that he was dragged out of the hole and left floating on top of the water. Soon the area is covered in blood. Two gunshots were fired and the coastguard patrolling boat left the area. A girl left her family house and walked into the nearby park. She picked up some flowers and sung as she danced. Abruptly she stopped and looked in front of her. A man was laying down. His eyes were closed. Oil like substances were leaking from his body. The girl turned around and quickly started running back to the house. After a while a young boy came out running followed by the girl and into the woods. The young boy without fear knelt next to the robot and checked what was wrong. "What's wrong with him? Is he going to be okay?"

Quizzed the girl. After a while the girl saw the crude oil leaking.

"Ew Yak! What's that?"

Queried the girl, Lily.

"Looks like black oil. I think he is hurt. Maybe we should call for help," suggested the boy, Jacob.

"Ew Yak! What's that?"

Repeated the robot, JT.

They all started laughing.

"He is mine I found him first. Let's take him inside the house."

Jacob tried to carry the robot JT into the house but he was too heavy. He tried everything but failed. JT was badly injured. Jacob ran inside the house to call for help. Lily stayed with JT.

"So, what is your name?"

"Hello pleased to meet you. I am."

"You are what?"

"Ew Yak! What's that?"

"Who?"

Questioned Lily smiling.

"I am JT."

"Where is your family JT? Where are your parents? Do you have brothers and sisters?" While she was talking, a strong wind is instantly felt and left leaves of trees scattered in the air. Lily covered her eyes. When she opened them again, she saw two more boys of same height and appearance. They carried JT before they disappeared upward.

"No! No! He is mine! Don't take him. JT! Come back!".

Lily slumped to the ground crying. Jacob came out running.

"What happened? Where is he? Where did he go to?" Lily with her twisted mouth pointed to the skies. Jacob looked at her sister.

"What?!"

He looked to the sky before sitting down next to his sister and hugged her.

CHAPTER FIVE

The Professor was in the lab analyzing the damage to JT when the lab doors swiftly opened. The Vice President entered the lab.

"What kind of incident is it Professor?" Inquired the Vice President. The Professor pointed at JT whose side was damaged. He was leaking oil. The Professor was wiping the oil from JT and the Vice President was watching too when JT spoke.

"Ew Yak! What's that?"

The Professor and the Vice President threw each other a quick glance.

"What does that mean?!"

"Mrs. Vice President. I think he had been in contact with some kids nothing to worry about. We can soon find out."

"What do you mean?"

Questioned the Vice President. The Professor did not reply he walked to the corner and retrieved some cables. He dragged then to JT and opened his naval area and plugged the cables. He looked at the monitor so as the Vice President. His last video soon after impact starts playing. The Vice President and the Professor looked at each other when they saw that he had head-butted someone and dragged him to the surface before plunging into the park.

"So, he records everything. Why was I not informed about this Professor?"

"This is the first of its kind. Just a trial project to be honest This is my idea. This is the only one fitted with such a mechanism. He only records when there is an impact. It's an impact sensor. Any collision, fighting, aggressive handling will activate the recorder, after that he then records the sound as well."

The Professor retrieved another cable and plugged it into the alien's naval. They heard the thump sound followed by the sound of a girl singing then later they heard another boy asking questions. The Professor played the impact video for some time.

"Don't understand why he was in the tunnel to the oil. My guess he saw the oil deposits. There will always be these. I think he might have followed the boy into the tunnel. Once JT collected the oil, he must fire all cylinders to counteract the heavy oil weight probably hence the collision."

"So, is he dead? Can he be a threat?"

The Professor typed coordinates on the keyboard. "See for yourself Mrs. Vice President."

A video shows the impact followed by the shooting and a satellite view showed him laying upside down. "There is no way he could have survived the impact. The speed at which JT was traveling any impact would have mashed his brain. JT was traveling at more than the speed of the light. He did not stand any chance. I sent out our boys just as a precaution." The President is in his office when the phone rang. He walked to his desk and picked up the phone. He later placed the receiver down and sat in his chair. He grabbed the TV remote and flicked the channels until he reached the news channel. He got up and sat at the corner of the desk and watched the news.

"In the neighboring countries sightings of an alien had been witnessed in recent weeks. The locals claim that an alien that looked like a small boy has been seen. It is believed that the boy had been seen flying into the sky at super speeds. No one has given concrete evidence about this. The President of the country concerned has addressed his countries fears and assured everyone that this was just a hoax. Chloe reporting for Touchladybirdlucky news. In the city center the Vice President and the Professor were watching the news in the office.

"The country and the world has been fascinated about the story of this young girl called Lily who claimed that she had witnessed alien invasion. Hear it from her." The anchor-woman turned and looked at the young girl and her brother standing beside her. "So, tell us what happened?"

Requested the anchor-woman Clarence.

"I found him when I was singing looking for flowers. He was bleeding some black oily stuff. I ran home and called Jacob but he couldn't carry him he was very heavy," explained Lily thrilled showing much enthusiasm.

"So, did he say anything to you?" asked Clarence. "Yes! Yes! Yes! He said, he said, eh, Ew Yak! What's that!"

The Professor looked at the Vice President with

wide-opened eyes. The Vice President stood up and walked toward the window.

"Can I send the cleaners?"

Inquired the Professor? In one of the neighboring countries in the capital city a car drove toward the city center. Amanda, a hot dark-haired girl with shining gray eyes got out of a sport luxurious red BMW wearing a short dress that revealed a rose tattoo on her left thigh and a gun tattoo on her right thigh. The music she was playing was the best of linking park. She removed the shades she was wearing as she walked to one of the city buildings.

"Woo is that you Amanda?" Ogles one of the man as Amanda passed by.

"Still same me Hinks, it's a shame you haven't got that face-lift done yet I could now be going out with you, you know?"

Bragged Amanda chewing gum.

"Pass, I am already taken." Shouted Hinks entering one of the offices. Amanda knocked a door and entered the office.

"Yes, I am glad you came. I have a new case. As a procedure, we must look at these cases straight away."

"Boss, I am already dressed up for my case. Why not ask Hinks to take this case? You can't change me the last minute." Complained Amanda looking frustrated.

"Hinks, is busy and a bit sloppy if you ask me. I want a professional on this one. This is a national security case. I want my best investigator on this one. You don't have to dwell on it. Find what you can find that's it. If the President is happy then I am happy too. Okay?"

"OK. Boss." answered Amanda taking the file and leaving the office. A red BMW sport car left the city heading toward the outskirts of the city. Amanda knocked a door and instantly the door was opened. "Woo that was fast. Are you expecting someone?" "No, are you a reporter?" Queried Holly.

"Not really, I am an investigator, national security. I would like to ask eh, Lily some questions if you don't mind."

"That's okay, I will go and check maybe she is asleep now. Has been a busy day with all the reporters." Explained Holly Lily's mother. Lily and Jacob came into the lounge area.

"What did this thing look like?"

"Looks like a boy, a real boy."

"So, why people think it's an alien, when it's a real boy?" Questioned Amanda.

"I think because the boy and his friends flew into the sky." Replied Lily.

"Pardon me you said with his friends? What friends there is no mention of friends in the report?" Jacob looked at Lily. Lily looked astonished and fascinated. Her face shone as she explained what had happened. "There was a gustily wind. I closed my eyes and when I opened them two more boys stood in front of me. They looked at me then at him and they lifted him up and all flew into the sky. I cried and cried. He was mine I found me."

"The other boys were they real boys as well?"

"Yes, real boys."

"In the report, you said that he spoke to you, you said, he said; Ew Yak! What's that?"

"He had this black sticky stuff coming out of him. Jacob touched the stuff, and I said Ew Yak. What's that. Then I asked him his name, and he repeated the same, and, and, he, said his name was JT."

"JT, sounds like an English word. I thought that maybe he couldn't speak English. So apart from flying this could be a real person."

"You can say that. My daughter always tells the truth." Quipped Holly sounding defensive.

"Has your daughter been sleeping well, having any problems, or wishing for a doll, that kind of stuff, I don't know anything?" Inquired Amanda.

"Not really, she had been herself obsessed with flowers though, lately apart from that just like any normal girl."

"Thank you for your time. One thing, can you show me where you found this JT."

Later that day Amanda was in the car going back to the city speaking on the phone with her boss.

"First impressions a hoax. Nothing whatsoever to do with aliens about the story. A real boy, he can speak English, tired girl, probably hallucinating the brother couldn't quite answer the fundamental questions about flying to the sky. But one thing disturbing about all this is the black stick-oily stuff. It's for real."

Later that day Amanda was in the lab. Alfie the lab technician was there with her talking about life before the subject changed to the sample results.

"So, aliens or not?"

"Come and look."

Amanda walked toward the desk and looked through the lens.

"What am I supposed to look at here, I am lost?"

"It's bloody oil, car oil, just not processed though."

"Crude oil, you mean?" Questioned Amanda.

"Who still uses the unrefined form?" Weeks or so after, Amanda was at the oil extracting and mining company near the coast.

"Any idea why someone would be needing raw crude oil? Any problems with theft?" asked Amanda.

"Not that I know of but you can never say never. Once I read somewhere that one of the co-worker, but not here though had a jacket that he used to fill with crude oil before taking it out of the mining."

A week or so after, Amanda is driving the car when her phone rung. She answered the phone and promptly slammed on the brakes and got out of the road into a lay-by. Later that day everyone was in the office, Hinks, his boss and the other guys and Amanda.

"Listen up, from today, Hinks Amanda is your partner stay together. Where ever she goes, you go too okay? Until we find out who is responsible for this." The Vice President's limousine was cruising going to the city center. As it approached, the city a group of people are marching to the center holding placards and posters. The limousine slowed down as the people were walking in the road. The Vice President was with her secretary Zoe.

"What do these people want Mrs. Vice President?"

"Stricter gun laws. They want licenses of all companies that continued production to be revoked. I know they have a point. We can use the penalty fees for something better. We did impose harsh penalties but still they continued with production. The limousine arrived at the government buildings in the city. The Vice President entered the building straight to her office. The phone rang.

"It's the President can I see you in my office." Later that day.

"I have finally approved and signed the delivery of the water carrying tankers most will be delivered by the end of the day Mrs. Vice President."

"Thank you, Mr. President, once the tankers had been delivered we can commence deliveries to the processing plant."

"Last night I saw a small boy outside my window and he just disappeared, is that part of your project? What are you not telling me?"

"Mr. President, you refused to be part of this project, but yes this is the project once we are up and running you will be the first to know."

"Does that have anything to do with sightings of aliens all over the world?"

"Once I think you are ready to know I will tell you. In the meantime, you will have a strong defense if I don't tell you and if you don't know, in case something goes wrong." The Professor was in the lab when the news bulletin was on.

"In a shocking and sad turn of events the girl who claimed to have seen an alien, has been found dead with her brother and mother. Her father is inconsolable. He is adamant that his family was killed. The police could not comment but sources close to the deceased family hinted that the national security officer visited the family days before they were all found dead. Lucia reporting for Touchladybirdlucky news."

"Damn!"

The Vice President was with potential investors when the Professor knocked at the door. He quickly entered the conference room.

"Do you have a minute? Something important has come up."

"Can that wait Professor, I am busy right now."

"I am afraid this can't wait Mrs. Vice President."

"What is it?"

"I think you must authorize phase four fast?"

"What? It's more than two years away from now?"

"Trust me, we might need it sooner, Mrs. Vice President."

"Don't scare me Professor what is going on?"

"OK follow me I will show you."

Later in the lab the Professor loaded the video. They watched JT doing his new job after his accident. Ever since he had been given a special role.

"As you can see the job was done perfectly."

The Professor played the news from the neighboring country channel.

"How did that happen?"

"We went in too late Mrs. Vice President. Only phase four will guarantee us that this will never happen. We have nothing to worry about everything is ready. Are you ready, Mrs. Vice President?"

"That will change everything overnight. I need time to think about this."

"Sure, when you are ready."

At a processing plant in one of the neighboring countries a young woman Liane entered her boss' office holding some graphs and charts.

"Sir, sorry for interrupting you but I think you need to see this."

"Can we go in the conference room better on the big screen?" Asked Steve.

"In that case I will be back I will go and grab my laptop."

"Yes, so, what is it?"

"I have been looking at production figures for the last 3 months there is something wrong." Steve looked at the graphs and after only a few seconds replied.

"I don't see anything wrong with this, we extracted and processed the target volume. Actual volume is nearly the same as the predicted volume. Why waste my time young Liane?"

"Sorry, Sir, it's in relation to the reserves." Steve walked to the screen and looked at the figures.

"You are right. How is that possible? Leave this with me I will check with the CEO Mr. Blinks later today."

A woman in a red short dress and black high heels fell to the ground. She quickly got up and looked behind her and then all around her. Her eyes' massacre had been messed up by the tears that her eyes looked like pandas'. She looked very frightened. She swiftly got up and tried to run with one shoe only in her leg. She removed the other shoe and ran barefoot. She screamed for help but there was no one. Her knees were bleeding. She slumped to the ground again touching her bleeding knees. The sight of the small boy running toward her petrified her to death. She quickly got up and ran for her life. JT stood still instantaneously and aimed at her. The girl instantly fell to the ground holding her shoulder. She looked behind her but the boy had disappeared. She searched everywhere, but the boy was gone. Or was he? She looked upward and saw the boy hovering in the air upside down just above her head. Swiftly he dropped down and grabbed her by the neck and lifted her up in the skies. She opened her eyes and sniveled with fear. She tried to look down but JT looked at her in the face.

"Ew Yak! What's that!"

Sarcastically quipped JT seconds before he changed into a small plane. Amanda first looked down as gravity beat her. JT looked at her as she was falling to the ground, it appeared as if it was in slow motion. She looked at the plane and waved her hands calling for help. Seconds later JT heard a heavy thump and Amanda lay on the ground with her legs next to her face and her eyes wide opened. She was bleeding from the nose, mouth ears and head. A passer-by ran to the scene. A loud scream sound echoed throughout the city. After work the CEO of the oil mine Mr. Chadwick Blinks was heading home in the neighboring country. He was given the production figures for the last months. Surely something was wrong. The road was very busy. He opened the file and looked at the figures while driving the car. The driver behind his car blasted his car horn when the CEO remained stationary. After a while the road started clearing up and soon he found himself on the road alone. Suddenly, his car went over something in the road. He pressed hard on the emergency brakes, and the car skidded stopping on the other side of the road. He got off quickly and ran in the road. He saw an animal breathing its last breath dying in the middle of the road. He sighed and walked back to the car. He looked in the rear-view mirror and was about to set off when he saw a boy in the road. He looked surprised as to where the boy came from. He got out of the car and looked back at the dead animal. He looked in front of him and the boy had disappeared. He got in his car and locked the doors. He sat there thinking that maybe he was hallucinating. He drove off and headed home. The phone rung sending him flying.

"Yes, Steve did you find out the probable reason?"

"I think the lost volume can be attributed to initial inaccurate readings. There is no way that the oil could have disappeared without anyone noticing."

"Alright thanks I will talk to the board of directors tomorrow." When he finished talking on the phone, he heard a sound as if someone had landed on the roof of the car. In front of him was that boy again. He looked in the rear-view mirror and saw another identical boy. On his side was another boy. He pinched himself. He looked at the boy in front of him. He slowly stopped the car and got out. The boy jumped upward and disappeared in to the clouds. The CEO quickly got into his car and locked his doors. He drove the car for some time looking around everywhere. The train sounded its horn as it approached the crossing. The CEO stopped his car as the gates were closing. The train now not far away the CEO patiently waited in his car. Soon after that his car rose from the ground and floated to the crossing. On lookers looked in horror as the CEO car landed on the tracks on the crossing. The train driver tried to stop the driver. The CEO struggled to get out of the car. Seconds before impact he saw the boy floating in the air. The time the train managed to stop, the car of the CEO was beyond recognition. People started dying mysteriously at the oil company after the CEO died. Steve the manager left the company. In another country, it's business as usual. People are going through their daily business. The city is vibrant, and the highway is packed with cars. A young driver driving a very expensive car entered a filling station. He filled his car a quarter full before the petrol ran out. He moved to another pump and filled to half the tank when the petrol ran out. He stopped and looked at the cashier inside. The cashier checked the meter and point to the other pump. After filling the petrol tank, he went inside.

"Hey are you running out of petrol or what? Why your pumps are empty?"

"Not sure why the meters are showing that, they are nearly half. We should have delivery yesterday. I wasn't on shift so I don't know if the tanker turned up or what." Replied the cashier. In a remote area of the country a drunken man was walking in the street late at night. He looked around and stopped for a while. He took out a bottle of whiskey from his jacket and drunk some. He threw the bottle away and proceeded his way. Later he felt a liquid going down his neck and head. He touched his neck and smelled his hands.

"Gasoline! It's raining gasoline?"

He looked up and saw a big lorry flying in the sky. Shocked and confused he slumped down onto the ground. He held his head and closed his eyes. He looked in the sky again. He saw the tanker flying in the sky. He got up and crawled in the road. Far away in the same country. A man in an expensive car entered the premises of a big company. He entered the building. Another man ran to him.

"Yes, Derek what seemed to be the problem?"

"Sir, I have been recently working with the chemical engineers and the scientist. For unknown reasons the API of the oil coming out now is less than 10*. We can't seem to pinpoint what changed. I think we must go back to the drawing board." Evans stopped for a while.

"How bad is it? On a scale of ten? Ten being the worst scenario."

"Honestly, Sir, eleven."

"That can't be right. The same conditions were to

prevail for the next six months per the forecast. OK I want everyone in the conference room now." Later that morning. Evans and the others are in the conference room, the CEO is addressing the meeting. "Ladies and gentlemen, I called this emergency conference meeting I understand all of you are aware of the situation we are in. I want to know the problems first hand from you before I meet with the board of directors."

"Costs will out weight any gains from extraction and processing. The oil is too viscid. To be able to sell it, we must mix it with the lighter oil. All this cost money." Explained Stacy the production manager.

"OK what is the worst scenario?"

"Closing down everything."

"What are the time frames? What is the forecasts?"

"Less than three months unless if you are injecting a lot of cash from somewhere."

Later that day Derek was home watching the news. The anchor-woman is talking.

"In an unprecedented turn of events the oil refinery and production has announced that it will close the extraction part and reduce the scale of operations. This is in line with the rising costs as the oil is now expensive to extract, refine and transport. This has hit hard the labor force and most will be surprised tomorrow when the board of directors announces job cuts starting from tomorrow. Thus, panic buying, has meant long queues all over the country. Asked when they will resume production, no one would say for sure. Susan reporting for Touchladybirdlucky news. The Vice President was at a dinner party with other members of the government. The President was there too as well as the Professor.

"Mrs. Vice President, have you heard today's news?"
"Not really Mr. President. What happened?"
"Soon there will be an oil war. Cost of production everywhere has meant the reduced production. Everywhere it's the same story. You choose water energy soon even us we will run out of fuel. Now it will be harder and expensive too to secure oil deals."
"I must admit it was a missed opportunity. In the future, we might get good deals. Whoever is going to buy must spend a lot of money to process and transport so patience might pay off in the end."
"You think so Mrs. Vice President?"
"Will be a blessing. We just need to secure and save a lot of money."

In another country after the closure of the extraction side of the oil mine a few people were left as compared to the glory days. Tito and Denise were going to work. Most of their friends had been made redundant. They were the lucky ones. They were in the car when Tito harshly slammed the brakes sending the car skidding narrowly missing the young boy in the road. "Damn! What is that kid doing in the middle of the road. I nearly killed him." The two got out of the car and walked toward the boy.

"Are you okay? Are you hurt in any way?" Tito touched the boy's head before he screamed in pain. "Let him go, it was an accident, he didn't see you." Denise looked in horror as his friend is lifted in the sky by his head. He saw him wriggling as the boy lifted him up in the air. Shocked and scared he ran to the car and started the car. About to drive away his friend's body dropped on top of the windscreen. His neck was longer than normal. In shock, he froze for a while. He quickly looked around and tried to drive.

He only managed to move a little when he saw two other boys floating in the air. After a while he wakes up to find himself airborne.

"Put me down right now! Who are you? What do you want?" He looked down to find that he was floating on top of the coastal waters. Suddenly, he was taken deep down under water. He struggled to breathe. The boy with the speed of lightning entered the tunnel underneath. Denise opened his eyes shortly before he lost unconsciousness. The old drunkard man walked into a local pub. He ordered a pint and sat on the long table. A man well dressed in a suit is having his meal and a pint of beer, his name is Mathew He looked at the man and continued with his meal. The drunkard man is called Francis. He looked at the television. He looked at the bar staff and pointed at the television.

"A lot of people have gone missing in the last month than in previous two years combined. Most suggest that the fuel shortages and the expensive cost of living has seen a huge out flux of people out of the country. So, those who might be recorded as missing might have actually gone to the neighboring countries." Annabel reporting for Touchladybirdlucky news.

"Soon all of us will be gone. I knew it. I told these people this was going to happen, but no one listened. The end of the world has come." The bar staff started laughing.

"You must be joking. Why is it every time we run out of a commodity everyone starts saying it's the end of the world? I don't get it. No money in this country, people simply go abroad. That's human nature. No one is missing or has been abducted like what I heard in the news." Francis looked at the bar staff and then at Mathew. He leaned close to Mathew.

"Aliens are abducting people if you ask me."

"What on earth made you say that?"

Queried the bar staff. "I just know it." Replied Francis.

"Maybe I should take that beer away from you," suggested the bar staff. Francis grabbed his pint and drunk his beer. He let out a big burp.

"Just last week when I was going home I saw a petrol tanker flying in the air." Francis did not finish talking as the bar staff and Mathew burst into laughter.

"This guy make me laugh. A flying tanker? That's a new one," confessed Mathew clearing his throat as the food nearly choked him when he started laughing. Francis drunk his beer.

"You two don't believe me? I swear the petrol tanker was flying." The bar staff couldn't stop laughing. "You know what? Today you have earned yourself a free beer. It's a long time since I laughed like this. Have you heard this guy? A flying tanker? You know what. I will get a pint for you now."

The bar staff walked to the counter and got a beer for Francis. Ray had just finished work when he arrived home. His girlfriend had cooked already. They had dinner and a glass of wine. Ray looked outside and saw a boy standing outside attentively looking at the house. He remembered seeing the boy outside at work.

"Hey there is a boy outside come and see. Velvet walked toward Ray and looked outside.

"Just a kid. Probably he kicked his ball in our yard. Or you might have left the upstairs television on."

"Maybe he is watching the television." Ray sat down

and later he went to observe if the boy was still there, but this time the boy had gone. Days after, Ray was driving home from work when he immediately saw the boy in the road. He swerved and his car hit the tree. He was injured and his head started bleeding. He looked in the rear-view mirror and saw the boy coming to him. He opened the door and tried to get out. He staggered outside.

"Hey are you OK? I didn't see you until the last minute. What are you doing here anywhere?" asked Ray. The boy jumped upward and flipped head down legs up floating in the air. Instincts kicked in and Ray ran for his life. The boy chased him upside down floating in the air. Ray had never felt this scared before. The chase continued. A car approached from behind him. The boy stopped but still airborne upside down. Ray ran in the middle of the road and tried to stop the car. The driver, a female, stopped the car and was about to open the door when the boy unexpectedly appeared in front of the car still upside down hovering. The driver quickly sped off leaving Ray stood. Another boy appeared and then another. Ray stopped and launched in the air whenever the boy was about to grab his head. Ray looked up and the time he looked down one of the boys was in front of him. The boy quickly took out a gun and instantly shot Ray in the head. He fell to the ground. One of the boys picked him up by the head and carried him to the coast. Mathew after having his meal drove home. He had this nagging feeling that somehow Francis story might have some truth in it. He stopped the car and called the local filling station.

"Just curious, did you have any delivery that was due but didn't turn up the past few weeks?"

"Hold the line I will pass you through to the manager he might be able to help."
"Yes, the manager speaking. How can I help you?"
"I was wondering if you had a missing delivery that never turned up?"
"We had one, but we got a replacement, they said it might have broken down on the way."

CHAPTER SIX

The Vice President was in her office when the Professor and his team entered the office and sat down. The Vice President stood up and walked to the window. She looked outside for a while before she walked back to her sofa.

"Ladies and gentlemen, I have called you today so we move forward with our plan. I want to know everything that can affect the plan before we move forward." She paused and looked at everyone.

"We must move forward as planned. I know its way early than planned but for some unforeseeable circumstances after speaking to the Professor and other interested parties I have made this decision to go ahead with the plan. Professor."

"Yes, Mrs. Vice President, I agree and everyone in my team agree too. It's going to be tough but we will stand by you all the way. Phase four can start now, a bit earlier than planned but I don't see any major issues."

"I think the number of the subjects requested for this phase is too high to cope with the resources currently available Mrs. Vice President. I personal think a lot need to be done first before we go on. Are you prepared for a world war in case something goes wrong? Do you have the security infrastructure to ensure secrecy and stealth operations?" Asked Abel the head of operations and security.

"I will have a word with the President first and get back to you all. You are dismissed."

Later that day the President and the Vice President are talking over dinner.

"I have been thinking. I think it's time we make the oil deal. Soon prices will rocket. Production worldwide has reduced and even stopped in some countries. My project is running fine enough to generate extra cash Mr. President."

"Well, we have to find out if they are still interested Mrs. Vice President." In the neighboring country, in one of the towns near the oil extracting sites a man is smoking outside. He looked up in the sky and the whole area. He finished smoking that's when he heard a thump sound as if something fell from the sky. He looked back and saw a boy standing just outside his yard. He looked up and when he looked down the boy had disappeared. "I do know what is going on. At one point, I thought I was losing it," explained Curtis.

"What makes you say that?" Asked Amelia.

"I thought I saw a boy outside but when I looked again, he had disappeared. All the stories about aliens, honestly I don't know what to believe anymore." Later that night Amelia was sleeping having a bad dream when she woke up.

"What's wrong, darling?" asked Curtis.

"Can't sleep well. I need something to drink." Amelia went downstairs. She entered the kitchen and found the boy laying on the floor with oil all over the floor. She ran back upstairs.

"Darling wake up there is an alien in the kitchen!" The couple ran downstairs.

"What shall we do? Maybe call for help," suggested Amelia.

"Maybe it's a real boy."

"A real boy are you crazy? Why would a real boy need all that oil for? Aliens I read that they take the form of human beings as well."

"Go and get my gun hurry up." Amelia rushed back in the bedroom and brought Curtis gun. He touched the boy slowly to wake him up. The boy slowly opened his eyes and scanned the whole place. He looked at his body and all the oil that was on the floor. He scanned the whole kitchen and quickly looked at the tape water. A droplet formed on the tape and as it grows, he watched closely and as the water droplet dropped the boy flipped in the air and quickly hovered to the sink basin and captured the droplet. Curtis instantly drew the gun and pointed at the boy. Still in air vertical but upside down the boy looked at Amelia and then at Curtis. Amelia sensed danger and she ran in front of Curtis pushing the gun away. The boy opened the water tape and looked at Curtis and Amelia. Curtis pointed toward the steps and up. The boy still upside down but vertical floated upstairs and entered the bathroom. The couple soon after heard the bathtub water running. Curtis threw a quick glance at Amelia. Curtis entered the living room and was about to call for help when Amelia stopped him.

"Think about it, by the time they will send help we might already be dead. If he meant harm he might have killed us. Put the gun away. We either just leave or try to talk to him."

"He is not human, aliens can't speak, I say we just leave." declared Curtis.

"Is he the boy you said you saw earlier on?" Asked Amelia. "I think so I didn't see clearly he disappeared after a short while."

"Maybe he wants something from you. Maybe it's God, giving us our son back?"

"Don't start Amelia. I told you not to talk about my son. We must move on."

"But darling what are the chances of something like this happening? Let's try to talk to him." Curtis and Amelia slowly went upstairs and slid open the bathroom door. The boy was in the tub fully submerged. He opened his eyes and looked at the couple who stood at the door. He simulated swimming and looked at the couple. Slowly they entered the bathroom. Curtis looked at the boy and put his hand in the water. The water was hot. He looked at the tapes. He got up quickly and ran downstairs into the kitchen. He got cooking oil and returned and poured the oil in the tub. The boy after a while stopped fidgeting.

"He was boiling. Look at the tape opened. It is that of the cold water but the water is hot. Oil seems to have done the magic."

"What's your name and what do you want."

"I am JT I want oil."

The couple relaxed after hearing that.

"Oil!"

They both shouted at the same time, looking at each

other. Curtis got in his car and drove to the shops to buy car oil and cooking oil leaving JT and Amelia together. JT returned after some minutes and entered the house.

"Darling I am back." JT ran upstairs and opened the bathroom. He found JT still in the bath twiddling. "Where is Amelia?"

He looked at JT before running upstairs in the bedroom and then spare room. He went downstairs and outside looking for Amelia. He came back in the bathroom.

"Where is Amelia? What did you do with her? Answer me or I kill you." Quickly JT looked around and then at Curtis.

"Oil I need oil."

"OK I give you oil first where is Amelia?"

"I take oil. Need oil. Hot."

Curtis pulled the gun from his back and a shot is fired instantly. Water started flowing out through the hole man by Curtis. JT is upside down next to him hovering in the air with water dripping down onto the floor. Later JT is laying down next to Curtis with his hand holding Curtis's body. On the floor oil is slowly moving from Curtis' body toward JT's. Steam came from Curtis body. His eyes look like fried fish's. A car left a house and entered the major road. A woman wearing glasses was driving the car. At the back seat was a young girl of school age.

"Mummy can you buy me a frog. My teacher brought one to school yesterday. I like it."

"Bev, last time you told me that I should buy you a Barbie now you want a frog?"

"I want both, I think a frog is very funny."

While driving a boy suddenly ran across the road and

fell to the ground. Gertrude quickly slammed the brakes of the car. She ran to the boy's rescue and put him in the car. Quickly she drove to the hospital. Days after a doctor went to the ward only to find out that the ward was nearly empty.

"Where are all the patients? Did they die? Or who discharged them?" Asked the doctor shocked and surprised.

"I was wondering the same myself too about that. I thought maybe you discharged them." Gertrude days after this incident was watching the news.

"Doctors and nurses were left baffled after they came to the hospital to find wards nearly empty. No one knew where all these patients went. One of the patient has insisted that an alien took all of them and flew with them to the skies. We have tried to trace some of the patients visiting their homes but relatives insist that they were still in the hospital. After some relatives accused the doctors of butchering their loved ones they visited the mortuary. This is a surprising story because even the dead people are missing too. We found relatives outside the mortuary waiting to take their dead loved ones for burial. The mortuary staff insist that they can't find them either. Christie reporting for Touchladybirdlucky news. Stories of people being abducted in the town near the oil mines circulated very fast. A big SUV car was driven by Alyssa and she is with the other girls, Caroline, Doreen, Ester and Hayley. They are going on a camping trip on the coast near the oil mine.

"Girls, aren't you scared about all these abductions and all these alien stories?" asked Caroline.

"Honestly I think it's all a hoax. I wouldn't pay too much attention to that."

After a while of driving Alyssa stopped the car and looked around.

"Why are we stopping here?" Queried Ester.

"I thought I saw a boy sitting over here. This is the second time now," revealed Alyssa.

"He could be an alien," suggested Doreen holding Hayley by the shoulders. Later the girls arrived at their camping house in the woods. They prepared food and talked about life and boyfriends. The following day they all went on an adventure to the coast. They climbed the local mountains and watched the whole area from the top. It was beautiful, they enjoyed the scenery. This was totally different from the city life they were used. "This is proper winding down, great scenery and plenty of fresh air unlike in the city." Alleged Doreen.

"Just imagine if you were free as a bird, you could fly anywhere in the world, visit any places you like and return the same day." Suggested Hayley.

"You can still do the Sam as a human you just need to have a lot of money," advised Caroline.

"What makes you say that Hailey?" asked Alyssa.

"Look over there since we have been sitting here I think I have seen that bird fly in and out of the ocean several times."

"What bird?" asked Ester.

"Look far over there on the sea waters."

"I think by afternoon we should have reached there. We should start going now girls."

They all left and headed to the shoreline. On arrival, they camped nearby and had something to eat. It was later after eating when they strolled to the seaside. It was very beautiful, clean water and a sunny day. They heard a large noise of something dipping into the

water and they looked over there but they did not see anything. They looked across the shore but there was nothing. Subsequently they saw a boy in the water. He looked real from that moment all the fear vanished.
"Are there people who live around here?"
"I think so, otherwise what would a boy his age be doing on his own here."
The boy vanished. Subsequently they heard something going out of the water from a distance. Alyssa looked using binoculars and quickly shouted to the other girls to look.
"What was that?" asked Carolina.
"Looks like a plane." Ensuing they were walking around the beach when they found skeletons. The girls felt afraid consequently they started heading home. They heard a big sound as if something dived into the water. They looked at each other and decided to go on high ground to check. Using binoculars, they saw a boy swimming before he disappeared. They remained watching when the boy reappeared and disappeared again.
"Is that a merman, as in mermaid?"
Inquired Doreen.
"Maybe alien?"
"Let's go back home it's going to be dark soon."
The girls rushed back home looking backward to see if anyone was following them. That night they all stayed in the bedroom and closed all the doors. Subsequently at night they were woken up by noises as if someone was trying to open the door. The girls opened their eyes and looked at each other. Alyssa got up and walked to the window and looked outside.
"That boy is outside come and see."
"He looks like a real boy."

"Aliens can imitate humans as well you know?" Replied Doreen.

"Stop scaring people, there are no aliens."

"So, if they are no aliens why are you scared to open the door. Maybe it's a boy in need."

"Don't open the door Hayley, please. I am scared." The boy dropped on the floor and started shaking. "What shall we do girls? Aliens don't do like that. Maybe it's a real boy who need our help."

"Not a good idea. I know now he is the same boy I saw the time I stopped the car. How did he get here so fast? Even if someone gave him a lift how did he arrive here?"

"Let's find out want he wants he is on the ground anywhere."

"Let's all go out there and find out."

The girls walked toward the boy. The all looked at him. They tried carrying him in the house but he was heavy. They subsequently took the boy in the house. "Oil I need oil."

"Oh, my God he can speak English!" Shouted Hayley. The girls relaxed after that. There wasn't enough oil in the house. The body kept shaking and after a while he touched Doreen. They all looked shocked as Doreen started boiling and steam started coming out of her mouth.

"Oil I need oil."

The girls when they saw what happened fear and shocked paralyzed them but consequently they found out their strength and started beating up the boy. The boy ensuing took out a gun and shot one of the girls. The rest of the girls ran outside. The boy lay next to the dead girl Doreen and extracted oils from her frying body. After a while he touched the other girl and his temperature begun to rise to a point the girls' inside started cooking. Oils dripped out and slowly moved to the boy's body. Caroline, Alyssa and Hayley jumped into the car and drove off. After a while smoke started coming out of the bonnet and the exhaust pipe. The car jerked before coming to a halt.

"What is the problem? Why are we stopping?"

"Oil, I think he took oil from the car."

Replied Alyssa.

"Maybe we should stay in here and lock ourselves in."

"I think we should keep ongoing on foot. We might get a lift from someone else. We stay here we will all die."

"But Alyssa that too far away, who can give us a lift this time?"

"What do you suggest then?"

"There is an oil refinery nearby we can go there and ask for help." They walked for some time following the signs to the oil refinery until they came along a cross road. They stopped for a while. The road to the oil refinery was very dark than the other roads. Fear struck them.

"We should continue, that's why we walked all the way here. We can continue with the other road but where is it going to take us? At least with this dark road we will know that we will get help. They proceeded along the dark road.

"Alyssa, can you hear that? There might be workers somewhere nearby. I heard voices," assumed Hayley. They walked for a few meters before they saw several shining eyes. The eyes seemed to have appeared from nowhere in a flash. They came across a group of boys in the road. As soon as they saw these boys, instincts kicked in, they ran as fast as they can. They looked backward, but the boys were not following at least in the road.

"Run, Hayley, run Caroline."

Hayley fell and Alyssa returned and picked her up. The girls ran for their lives until they reached the cross roads. They saw the headlights of a car coming their way.

"Hayley look."

"A car let's stop it and get a lift.!" Shouted Caroline. The girls started jumping up and down in the middle of the road.

"Look out!"

Shouted Caroline. The car knocked down Alyssa and nearly killed Hayley too. Horrified and lost for words, the girls for a while just looked in disbelief. Instantly it became apparent that death was imminent. Subsequently, the girls heard noises in the sky. They looked upward and instantaneously froze with fear. The boys were all upside down but vertical and staring at them with piercing scintillating eyes. Alyssa lay in the road bleeding next to them. The girls looked at each other instinctively got up and ran for their lives. A swarm of boys landed on Alyssa and they drained all her oil so fast fighting to have a drip of her best oils. They all rose above the ground and for a while hovered on top of her dead body, the tarmac had partly melted and Alyssa's body looked cooked and the tarmac glitters with her oils. Caroline and Hayley ran in the middle of the road constantly looking backward and in the air. Moments later a swarm of boys passed them in the air sending them ducking on the ground. Subsequently they saw the car that had passed them flying in the air carried by the boys, they prodded and hugged each other. After the car, had passed above them they ran, tumbling, and getting up. A car stopped in front of them going in the direction they had come. They gave each other staring glances and snubbed a lift after the driver refused to go back the other way. As the driver passed them he looked in the rear-view mirror and saw a swarm of boys carrying the girls into the air. Mathew is in the hotel lobby waiting to check-in when the anchor-woman appeared on the television. "Footage had been released showing strange birds many feet high up circulating in the skies. This has been shot by one of the plane passengers who caught a glimpse of the swarm. All the experts are saying no such birds have been known to fly that high. This is the first-time scientists have noted such bird behavior. Some are saying that they are not a swarm of birds but a group of aliens. We have sent footage to some experts so that they can analyze it. Penny reporting for Touchladybirdlucky news." At a command base in the neighboring country, the general entered the office. The two men left the office and headed to another room full of state-of-the-art equipment.

"Yes, what is it general?"

"There has been some strange activity in the skies recently or should I say we have recently noticed this."

"What I don't understand is this; is this the same picture that has been taken several times or what?"

"That's what we thought too. The truth is that all these images were taken at different times and different days."

"What kind of bird's feeds from one area all the time.? What do you know about the area?"

"Good rich place for birds to look for food. Only that the activities have intensified a lot recently. Maybe it's worth checking out."
"Jurisdiction issues, we will need permission to go in that area. Until I get authorization, I would suggest you don't send anyone there."
"What if I am going on a vacation?" "At your own risk, nothing to do with me then it's up to you."

CHAPTER SEVEN

The Professor was in the laboratory when he heard a knock on the door before he answered it the Vice President entered the lab.

"What appears to be the problem this time Professor?"

"Mrs. Vice President there are a lot of things we don't know about, yet things we must learn one day." The Professor moved to the table and inserted some memory card before an image appeared on the screen. He looked at the image and then at the Vice President.

"Yes, what does the image of birds have to do with our project? You said this has something to do with the project. I am very busy and when you know what you are doing. Then come to my office."

Upset the Vice President turned around about to leave.

"Mrs. Vice President, just a few minutes. Just look."

"What?"

The Professor smiled and looked at the Vice President. The Vice President walked closer to the screen and looked at the Professor.

"What's this how is this possible." Asked the Vice President.

"Shocked myself Mrs. Vice President. There are huge implications for this."

"Did you program them to do that?"

"No, I mean they are programmed to learn, adapt, and adopt

"So, what implication does this have on our project?"

"Huge implications. In terms of time and resources. They are spending more time now in groups flying than with the extraction of oil and above all they are using oil to fly all the way up there. There is competition for resources between you and them now and this can be a problem in the future."

"How can we correct this Professor?"

"Rewrite the program and reinstall the software all takes time, money and delays the project."

"What I don't understand is why the birds."

"Evolution, they fly like the birds so one day they followed the birds and now they fly in swarms and does everything together."

"Any dangers? They seem to be going in the wrong direction."

"If they are fully evolved will you be able to control them without resorting to butchering them?"

"I think we should move to phase five now."

"Professor phase five is three years away from here. We don't have the infrastructure yet for phase five. I am not even in full power yet how is that possible?" Mathew after getting a copy of the footage of the flying birds captured by a passenger in a plane he headed out of the city. He drove for miles before he came to a house in a remote area. He heard the barking of a dog coming from the house. He entered the property and a lady in shorts stood at the door. As he approached the door, a dog came out running and the lady shouted its name as she tried to hold it. "Don't worry about the dog you should be alright." They had dinner and a glass of wine before they headed downstairs. They entered the basement which had state-of-the-art equipment, computers and a big screen

"That's where Jones spends most of his time playing games. So, what did you bring me?"

"Not sure what it is, can you look at this?" Mathew handed the tape to Norah. The pixels are not good it will be hard to get a clear image on this.

"What happened? You never had a job too big or too small? Where is that girl?"

"That was a long time ago Mathew. I will try but I can't promise. What do you think it is?

"Honestly, confused, I have this nagging feeling that won't go away. I met this old drunkard. He told me that he saw a fuel tanker flying in the sky. Trust me, I laughed at him as if my ribs were going to break. Then came the fuel crisis and all the alien thing. I am thinking what a coincidence. One day I phoned the filling station. Boom they were missing a delivery."

"The tanker could have broken down Mathew."

"That's exactly what they initially said. Weeks later I requested them to check if they now know for sure if it had broken down." Mathew paused and took a glass of wine and drunk some.

"So, what did they say?"

"The tanker up to now is missing. No trace what so

ever and you know what the sad part is?"

"What?"

"The lorry driver was a married man up to now no one knows where he is."

"Did you speak with his wife?"

"She said that he ran away with another woman and maybe sold the fuel abroad."

"OK, let's see if we might be going somewhere with this. So, what's with this footage you think these are not birds?"

"Aliens maybe."

They both laughed.

"Aliens ah, that will be something."

It took more time than they thought. Mathew slept in the basement and Norah went to her bedroom upstairs. In the morning, Mathew woke up and powered on the computer monitor that had gone on sleep mode. He looked shocked.

"Norah! Norah!"

He ran upstairs and found her door opened. He slid the door open and looked inside. Norah was kind of cooked and the floor was glittering with her oil. He quickly ran downstairs and found the dog fried to death too. He went outside straight to the car subsequently he saw a swarm of boys on the roof top flying up and down moving and changing places. He looked at the car door keyhole first and when he looked up again, he felt the most excruciating pain on his shoulder. One of the boys had bitten him very hard. They all flipped upside down and hovered in the air toward him from the roof of the house. Stacy was excited that she was meeting her boyfriend later that day at the airport. She had waited for him for some time now. At last they have a chance to be together.

She arrived early at the airport and waited. She sat down and looked at the control tower. She imagined what it would be like to work in there. Outside, the tower was oval with glasses surrounding it. Inside were various stations and tables with computers and monitors. There was a big screen in the middle and Adam was in the tower. He took binoculars and looked all around. Chantelle was sitting facing oncoming traffic together with other member of staff. A pilot of one of the plane requested an emergency landing.

"We require emergency landing, under bird attack engine one possible failure."

In the cockpit, the pilots are struggling to control the plane in mind air. They had seen a swarm of birds and after some time the birds disappeared but one of their engine failed. A boy was sitting next to the window on the plane when he suddenly gazed at his mum.

"Mummy look there is a boy outside, look mummy."

"What boy?" Queried her mum looking outside the window. She instantly pressed the help button. It took longer than usual for the air hostess to answer the call for help.

"What seems to be the problem?"

"There is a boy outside the plane?"

"No, we had birds problem but nothing to worry about. We spoke to the pilot everything is going to be alright."

"But it was a boy I saw him by my own eyes it wasn't any bird. I swear my son saw the boy too."

"It's okay, I will speak to the pilot."

In the cockpit, the pilots are working very hard to keep the plane flying. The air hostess entered the cockpit. "Keep the passengers calm we switched off one of the engines. I saw birds flying toward us, I was afraid that the birds might damage the engine." Explained the pilot.

"One of the passengers said that she saw a boy outside the plane," revealed the air hostess.

"At this altitude, I don't think so, anywhere go and sit down we are preparing for an emergency landing." The plane started vibrating, and a boy hovered in front of the cockpit window upside down folding his leg.

"What the hell is that!?"

The pilots looked dumbfounded and terrified at the same time. They aborted the emergency landing. They switched on the second engine and braced for the worst. Initially, engine two started causing the plane to shake and vibrate before the plane ultimately stabilized. The other boy appeared instantly, so as the other, then another after that, until a swarm of boys encircled the plane. Everyone in the plane looked outside. The boys looked like air sky divers wearing same clothes and doing everything simultaneously. When the plane was over the sea, the boys vanished.

"What happened? Where did they go?" Everyone looked outside the windows searching for the boys. Suddenly the emergency alarms became activated in the cockpit. The oxygen masks instantly were ejected in front of the passengers. A constant alarm was activated throughout the plane.

"What's going on?" Quizzed one pilot to another. "Losing altitude unexpectedly fast, seemed we are being forced down."

"Try to gather altitude quickly, deactivate autopilot." Frantically the pilots did their best. They tried gaining altitude but unfortunately somehow the force was too much and subsequently the plane plunged into the sea the pilots saw a boy looking at them through the cockpit screen. The pilots had no time to radio the tower. In the tower, Chantelle got up and signaled the senior air traffic controller.

"We have lost flight X. It just disappeared from the radar." Any distress calls?

"Yes, they radioed the tower reporting engine failure Sir."

"Why they didn't land down?"

"Last time they radioed the tower they acknowledged that they had regained the engine and that everything was okay." Far away a man came out of a house and stood outside smoking. He looked upward and saw a group of birds up in the sky circulating. He looked again closely. The birds looked strange for some reason. He smoked his cigarette and the dogs started barking. He was about to enter the house when one of the boys flew down at lightning speed and grabbed his head and flew back upward instantaneously. He wriggled as he was being taken upward. The other boys started circulating him pushing each other in mid-air. They all grabbed him in midair before descending with him. They roasted him just by touching him and drained all his oils out of him. The door to the house opened, and a man shouted looking outside.

"Alfred! Alfred! Where are you Man? This is not funny you know? Come out now," shouted Yanka. He came out of the property yard and looked around. That's when he saw a pile of boys pushing each other. Scared and shocked he whistled, and the dog came out running.

"Go get. Go boy!"

The dog ran as fast as it can to the scene but as soon as it arrived the swarm of boys hovered up in the sky instantly with one of the boys grabbing the dog and lifting it very high. The dog barked viciously for help. The boy released the dog in mid-air and in as if in slow motion the dog is beaten by gravity. Yanka screamed in horror on seeing this and ran to catch the dog before it falls to the ground. Just about to catch the dog he found himself in the air being carried up. He heard a huge thump before looking down and shrieked. His turn to tumble subsequently arrived, all the boys looked at him as he fell. A woman in the house heard the commotion and went outside. She witnessed Yanka hitting the ground very hard. She hadn't seen the boys up in the sky. She instantaneously started running toward Yanka before she heard a buzzing sound. She looked up and saw these creatures flying down toward her. She stopped and turned running back to the house. Some boys followed Yanka to the ground, but a few waited for fresh meat. Ensuing, roasted bodies of Yanka the girl, Alfred and the dog were carried away. The Vice President was in her limousine going to the city center from a business trip. Her phone rang and she answered the call. Later that day the Vice President was still in her office but this time taking to the Chief Security Officer. A sharp knock on the door signaled the end of their conversation. The Chief Security Officer left, and the Professor came in. He opened his laptop and showed a clip to the Vice President. The Vice President looked at half of it and looked at the Professor.

"Why the plane? We are in the oil business? What's going on Professor?" Questioned the Vice President.

"Honestly in this instance I have no clue. My assumption is that they want refined oil. If you remember clearly, the first subjects when they absorbed unprocessed crude oil they fell asleep for hours incapacitated."

"Are you telling me that they have realized that crude oil is not good for them? Professor we are dealing with robots not some genius human beings."

"I thought so too until I saw this."

The Professor played another video clip and soon afterward the Vice President looked in disbelief.

"I don't believe this. I asked for robots that can extract oil and not some hungry carnivores."

"It's not the flesh they are after. No. Look very closely, Mrs. Vice President."

The Vice President looked at the video again.

"They are cooking them, why?"

"Human oil, is the only guess." Replied the Professor. The Vice President terrified and shocked stood up and walked to the window. She looked outside for some time before coming back and sat down.

"How does this affect our program?"

"They are evolving and they don't see any reason why they should spend the whole day extracting oil. They have stopped consuming the crude oil, which is a good thing as we need the oil. They have divided themselves into groups. They have selected a leader it seems. Extraction is now timed but still extracts same amount out as usual. Most of their time they spend hunting for humans."

"Have we not created creatures that will kill us all in the end?"

"My worry was competition for crude oil but I am shocked they have developed tastes for human oil.

Are we heading for extinction or not I cannot answer that?"

"We might actually use them, to advance my agenda years earlier. I understand we are to release the second batch few months from now, yes?"

"Correct, Mrs. Vice President. What I don't know is whether the new batch will stick to crude oil first or copy these to human oil."

"What's the worst and best scenarios?"

"The worst scenario is when they will eliminate humanity faster than we thought. The best scenario is when you can use them to obliterate your enemies without anyone knowing. Just program them to a certain zone and let nature take itself."

"OK I will need the President's approval I guess I have to talk to him straight away."

The President just arrived in his office. He walked to the cabinet and took out wine. He poured some and looked outside the window. He remembered the day a boy nearly gave him a heart attack. The phone rang and he answered the call. Soon afterward the door opened and the Vice President entered the room. "Mrs. Vice President what a pleasant surprise I was just thinking about you. What brings you here?"

"Thank you, Mr. President. I have business to talk about."

"Sit down Mrs. Vice President?"

"Mr. President there is something I must tell you. Please sit down."

"OK. I am listening."

"We have a problem. My project didn't go per plan."

"I thought you nearly repaid the loan? What is the problem?"

"It's not about the money. Loan nearly repaid. It is

what was on the news that is a matter of concern if you have heard regarding the missing plane."

"What does that have to do with you Mrs. Vice President?"

"We need to move to phase five and I need your approval. I will get the funds from the investors and clear the loan in full but I need your authorization."

"Mrs. Vice President you asking me to sign my life away. I don't know much about this project and it's my neck on the line."

"The more you don't know the better when time comes you will know everything."

"OK, let me think about this overnight and we will talk again tomorrow." In another country troops are running carrying guns and they are heading to a crash site. A jet fighter plane had just lost control and crashed. The pilot had sent distress signals that he was being attacked. The country was alert and news spread of a likely alien attack. The soldiers crawled in the forest as they approached the crash site. They searched the world area and found the pilot alive. He had subsequently ejected just before the crash.

"Are you okay?"

"My leg I think it's broken."

"I mean who attacked you?"

The pilot quickly looked everywhere and upward petrified. He looked scared.

"Let's go it's not safe here."

"Don't worry we are here now. Still you didn't answer my question. Who attacked you Soldier?"

The pilot looked up in the skies and pointed his finger.

"Soldier are you okay?"

The soldier whispered in another soldier's ears and

both man started laughing. The pilot kept looking upward as he limped away carried by the soldiers. Other soldiers arrived and took cover while others searched the area. They all gazed up in the skies.

"What did they say? People in the tower?"

"They said that he sent a distress call; alien attack."

"What did he tell you?"

"Nothing he just pointed to the sky."

The newly arrived soldiers scanned the sky and called each other.

"What is that up there?"

"Looks like birds?"

"Aliens!" Shouted the pilot.

One of the soldiers aimed his gun upward and cursed harshly firing bullets. Instantly the swarm in the skies dispersed forming a circle.

"For sure they are not birds. Take cover! They are coming! Open fire!"

All the soldiers ducked down. As the aliens approach they but opened fire. The group instantly changed directions and positions flipping from left to right but still descending. They scanned the ground and instantly flew back upward. The soldiers fired shoots again. The swarm descended at swift lightning speeds. At close range, the soldiers all opened fire. After locking down all the soldiers' positions on the ground the swarm descended for a bloody kill. Positions locked, the swarm swift and precise the soldiers had no chance. They died the time they let the swarm lock their positions. The second descend was such a bloodbath that no soldier survived. I mean, only the pilot was lucky maybe it had something to do with the fact that he can fly a plane. No one knows nevertheless the pilot instantly grasped that his existence was not out of luck but a matter of their choice. He ran for his life. The country prepared for war and this was all over the news. When another group of soldiers came, they did not find any bodies or guns but they saw blood spots. The aliens had vanished. In a shop window a woman stood outside watching the news.

"The country is preparing for a war. It became apparent that an undisclosed number of soldiers were killed by the aliens today. This is not a hoax as one pilot has escaped. He is currently receiving medical treatment as we speak. The President has spoken on national television asking the people to stay indoors. Michelle reporting for Touchladybirdlucky news."

A van is driving along the road and after a while entered the yard to a house in a remote area. The side door of the van opened and two men with guns got out of the van and entered the house. Another man with a briefcase followed them. The doors of the house were not locked the house was empty. They searched the house and found what they were after. They carried the boxes with the guns into the van and soon afterward the van drove out of the yard and disappeared. The van entered the garage of a house and a man entered the house. He sat on the couch and watched the news. "Panic and chaos have spread all over the city. Long queues have been forming all day. This time it's the gun shops that are flooded unlike last months when people were after food. Things have changed. When faced with such a situation mankind resort to buying guns. But many had flooded the airports taking the first flight away from this country. Whatever it is it has caused panic and fear among the local inhabitants. Jennifer reporting for Touchladybirdlucky news." At a barracks, soldiers are matching and forming queues. They form lines before getting to a military van. Once it's filled the van departs, they waited for another van to arrive. That has been going on for some time now. Among them is a young soldier still on training seventeen or eighteen. He looked inside his helmet and took out a picture of his mother and looked at the picture. He put it back and looked ahead of him. Across him is another soldier. He looked relaxed and very confident. He looked at the young soldier and sensed fear. He looked at the badge on his breast pocket and touched it before looking at the young soldier. Back at the base one of the soldiers was still at the base camp. In fact, he was still in the dormitory. He had panic attacks. He had a brown bag on his mouth. He sat down. The doors of the dormitory suddenly opened.

"Ernest let's go!".

The soldier quickly took his gear and ran out of the dormitory and into the queues.

CHAPTER EIGHT

"Sorry to interrupt Mr. President but it's a matter of national security."

"OK. Leave us."

Ordered the President talking to potential investors. They all left the office and closed the door behind them leaving the President and the Vice President to talk. "What's the urgency Mrs. Vice President?" The Vice President walked to the table and grabbed the television remote and switched on the television. "The nation is on alert and going to embark on a war with the aliens. These aliens occupied their land. The President informed the nation that he had used his Presidential powers to declare a war against the aliens. The leaked footage shows the aliens circulating up in the skies." The Vice President switched off the television and looked at the President.

"I need the approval straight away. Those are my subjects. If any get caught we are doomed. They all have serial numbers all linked to us." The President looked flabbergasted and gazed at the switched off television before looking at the Vice President.

"So, that boy on my window too and those boys yours?"

"Yes, Mr. President all mine."

"I don't see the problem let them fight for you. I never thought about that. So, what do you want? Mrs. Vice President?" The Vice President walked to the window and stood there for a while before coming back.

"I need your approval so that I can start phase five."

"What is this phase five?"

"Phase where our military capabilities are highly developed. I need authorization to command the soldiers in this phase. This is for our own national security."

"I am here and I am the President if anything happens I will be responsible for executing orders."

"I know that but we implemented phase four years earlier without the infrastructure to support it. The subjects' development was very fast than anticipated. If we are to be attacked, we won't stand a chance to defend the subjects."

"Mrs. Vice President you are not being honest with me. I might be old but I am not stupid. OK once again tell me what is on your mind."

"OK Mr. President you want the truth I will tell you the truth. I have invested billions of dollars building my project and I am not going to sit and watch another country destroy my project. Billions have been injected into this project and I will do whatever it takes to protect this project. So, I need this authorization in case we need to defend our billions."

"I am listening."

"These subjects are less advanced than the phase five subjects. These are not made for war. They are like miners not soldiers they need my protection. They are just extractors and collectors. This war is going to destroy all my work and our future. You have seen what they are like. The best thing any President can wish for if they had the guts and foresight to see the future."

"So, you want to start a war? When were you going to tell me about all this?"

"Not starting a war Mr. President but defending what is rightfully ours. They are my boys. I can't let them get killed. No. When time was right I was going to tell you. It's only that everything is happening so fast but surprisingly fascinating."

"So, in this world of yours am I in there and who am I?"

"The President still," answered the Vice President saluting before continuing.

"These subjects are now our future soldiers I want you in our future world. The boys need you and together we shall rule the world. Approve phase five so that we can release the real war subjects. Anything goes wrong it will be covered under executive Presidential powers and everyone will have immunity." The President got up and walked to the window and looked outside.

"Where do you get the balls to do all that? Sometimes I wonder Mrs. Vice President. I will approve phrase five with immediate effect. Anything else you want?" The Vice President smiled and handed the papers to the President to sign. The army general is in front of the office addressing the soldiers everyone else is listening attentively

"We have increased concerns over the identified satellite activities. Months ago, an alert was raised, but we did not take it seriously because it was not in our jurisdiction. But today it's different. Alien threat knows no borders so I say today we prepare for anything coming our way. I will talk to the President today after this meeting. Look what is happening in the neighboring country. We must be prepared as well."

"General I want to point out that the activities over the oceans has increased in the last weeks, whatever is going own there is no good. You can have a look." The lieutenant general switched on the wall projector that showed satellite movements in and around the oceans.

"It looks like some birds' activity but our specialist denied that weeks ago, and now we know for sure that this is an alien activity. Who knows we might be next. What do they want, is anyone's guess?"

In another country, the soldiers are traveling toward the coast lines going to fight the war with the aliens. A chain of military vehicles lined up the road as the helicopters fly over. So many vans and tankers headed toward the coastline. On the front line the soldiers are waiting for war. Fighter jets have been scrambled as well. All over the news it's about this war. People are watching in their homes gathered together. This is not like any war. Previous footage of birds like aliens up in the skies is constantly shown on the television. As soon as it got darker a whistling sound is heard above the soldiers and the chain of vehicles lining up the road. A swarm of the aliens passed on top of their enemies at more than lighting speeds. A second wave followed the first just seconds apart. Some soldiers were inside the vehicles and most were walking on their sides going ahead.

"What's that?" Shouted one soldier to another. "Jesus! It smells like gasoline."

For most no one realized what was going on. Unexpectedly, the whole line of soldiers was up in flames. Vehicles with weapons exploded finishing off the soldiers on the ground and inside them. Almost everyone was on fire burning. Those lucky few who had escaped were sprayed for the second and third rounds with lightning speeds some even for the fourth round until they succumbed and died. In the two thousand history of mankind no one has witnessed such a thing. People at home watching the television felt sick and their stomach churned. By the time the jets fighters arrived everyone had been roasted. It was not over yet, the aliens were still showing off their lethal skills, as the jet fighters unaware of the situation, were sprayed with oil as well and set on fighter by the swarm of boys who swiftly descended and carried all the dead soldiers up in the air one after the other. Soon afterward the cleaning begun. Send in the cleaners how fittingly? Fear spread throughout earth. This day mankind died. The world witnessed alien lethal skills and fury as soldiers got obliterated in seconds and cleaned off from earth. Every human being who watched this knew that the end had come. A nation was brought to its knees in seconds. What petrified the people the most and left them thunderstruck was the taking up of the dead soldiers into the skies before the swarm of boys disappeared. In chaotic manner and swiftly the people took the few things they can carry and headed toward the airport. It was like an animal pandemonium out of the country. The old and the young alike all rushed out of the country. The oil mines and everything was all abandoned. Most people can accept the notion of dying but very few will agree to the concept of being part of a food chain as well. Mankind died this day the country was deserted. In the whole region fear was written on everyone's forehead. The neighboring countries sent fighter jets and at first sight all the swarm of boys turned into smaller jets ten times faster than their jets and disappeared. When they returned as a swarm of boys the scrambled jet fighter pilots saw the boys pissing oil all over their fighter planes before they disappeared in a flash. Only returning for a second piss before setting them ablaze. One of the new models of the boy robot fell in the ocean because of overheating and the others brought oil for and left the robot in the deep waters of the sea. The President after watching what had happened on the news sent for the Vice President. Hours later they are in the office. The president's usher knocked the door and announced the arrival of the Chief of National Security.

"Tell him he has to wait for some time." Yelled the President sounding upset.

"Yes, Mr. President. You called for?"

"Yes, Mrs. Vice President."

He paused and took a long breath trying to contain anger. He looked really upset and was shaking. He glanced at the Vice President with staring sharp eyes like a hungry lion. The Vice President looked calm though but a bit concerned.

"When I authorized phase five, that's not what I had in mind. You said that you wanted to protect your boys and retrieve them. The aliens are attacking the neighboring countries. Surely that's barbaric. I have never seen such a horrific and gruesome scene all my life. The whole army obliterated in seconds."

"In order to lead you must project an image of bravery and ruthless. Soldiers die Sir. This is not a game. This is war. We choose how to fight this is how I want to fight. Zero casualties from my side. Did you see that? Wait until you have witnessed phase Six? This is just the beginning."

Instantaneously the President threw a quick angry stare with his eyes wide opened as if saying; are you mad?

"You must be out of your mind Mrs. Vice President? Stage Six. I won't authorize anything like that again. I am not a murderer. Don't taint my name. I am a good person. What do you think the international community will say? Do you want to die in jail? You think you can get away from something like that?"

"I don't see why not? What international community are you talking about Mr. President?" The President instantaneously got up and looked at the Vice President with deep red eyes. For a while they locked their eyes together. The President shocked by the arrogance of the Vice President walked toward the window trembling in fear this time. Clearly this was no laughing matter. This was war. The President opened his cabinet and took out a wine bottle and poured some.

"This is beyond human circles. Mrs. Vice President do you want to be God? No mankind has done want you have done today. The whole country deserted."

"There is always first-time for everything Mr. President, and it starts with me."

"Why this country Mrs. Vice President if I may ask?"

"Mr. President that is a question for phase six. When time comes, I will give you an answer, now I am in the dark as much as you."

"Mrs. Vice President this is the real reason I called for you. Will they know that it's you, it's us?" Interrogated the President putting the glass of wine down. He looked attentively at the Vice President.

"I am here to make a statement. I have nothing to be afraid of. In the end, every human being on earth will know but as for now I think it's best if we keep it a secret. After the incident, we had with subject JT, we have made the project anonymous. And to answer your question. Aliens belong to another planet so clearly that has nothing to do with us. Did I answer you satisfactorily Mr. President?"

"Crystal clear Mrs. Vice President we shall talk again soon. I have to talk to the Chief of National Security."

The Vice President got up and walked a few steps toward the door about to leave when she walked back in.

"This might be a major war, we might need guns maybe use your executive powers, you know?" She raised her eyebrows and looked at the President. "But, Mrs. Vice President, I have seen with my own eyes on the news what happened today, surely you don't need any guns?"

"I know, Mr. President, I mean for them. We might as well make money while we are on it after all it will look a bit fair don't you think? So far it's one-sided?" She turned around and walked out of the office and into her limo and disappeared. Later that day the Vice President was in her office. She picked up her phone and dialed the Professor.

"Can we talk I have some important information I want to tell you?"

"Yes, Mrs. Vice President in fact I wanted to see you I am actually on my way to your office as we speak."

"That's great see you soon." Later that day.

"Yes. Professor you first."

The Professor opened his brief case and took out his laptop and documents. "We might have suffered a causality on one of the new models. If I am correct, I think it just overheated and dropped in the ocean to cool down or the worst-case scenario is that it has been shot down. Apart from that I think that's the fastest an army has been obliterated from earth in human history. Congratulations Mrs. Vice President. Wait until you have witnessed the subjects in phase six. The world is yours Mrs. Vice President."

"Can that subject be recovered?"

"I issued a command to retrieve but command was overridden." Stunned and surprised.

"Has someone hacked our system? Overridden by who? I thought all follow your commands?"

"This is evolution Mrs. Vice President. The aliens now assess risks as well themselves."

"Isn't that a sign of a future problem?"

"You can say that but they will never break the first rules so as far as we are concerned we should be okay."

"Any footage of the incident. I don't want anything to go wrong. I have persuaded the President to approve phase five and begun gun production to sell abroad."

"Gun production I thought?"

"Yes, but we have used Presidential powers to start production with immediate effect. That brings me to the main reason I called you."

"Yes, I am listening."

"I want a satellite image of every country's weapons base or bases as of today, I want 100% accuracy. Once you have the positions, then let me know."

"Mrs. Vice President, what you are asking me is beyond what is in my contract."

"I see, we can write another contract, with new terms."

"Eh, you were saying?"

"Yes. I want all the satellite positions of all weapons stocks and send our boys everywhere tonight without failure okay?"

"Okay."

A small baby walked in the city center staggering following her mother. The mother stopped and waited for the baby to arrive before carrying her and kissing her. An old man is sitting across the bench he looked at the child and mother as the two share some intimacy. He smiled and for some time forgot all his worries. He had been coming to this mall and park bench for as far as he can remember. The mall wasn't there though. This mall was recently built. Long time ago there used to be a banker here. The recent development has seen a lot of changes in the city. This day was like any other day. Everyone running around their way, minding their business. Shoppers with money were shopping in the mall and the workers were busy earning money working. A swarm of boys flying in the skies came from nowhere and drenched the mall and part of the park with highly flammable raw oil. Seconds later the saddest scene you will ever see unfolded. Kids with their parents burning to death. Calls for help as people burn to death were sent all over, but the response wasn't swift enough. As soon as the victims had succumbed and fallen down the boys would swiftly come and collect them. People looked in horror as the mall went in flames. No one knew what this was about until after the fire was at its peak. The explosions said it all. It was like in a middle of a war, with bombs exploding and the burning pullets explodes as well. Sounds of bullets exploding sent people into panic and ducking for their lives. In every major country, all weapons bases were set on fire and in some countries the vehicles as well. The President and the Chief of National Security were in the office when they watched the weapons bases go ablaze. This was worldwide. In all countries, there were no civilian causalities apart from one of the countries where more than one hundred civilians died when the mall they were in was set on fire. The angry Vice President entered the Professor's lab. She paced up and down. Breathing heavily and her face filled with anger and rage.

"Kids and women Professor? How come? I made it clear that 100% accuracy at least you should have come and talked to me first. That is not excusable. That jeopardize the project and any future assaults It's way too early for such errors. Causality deaths carry a heavy burden it's too early for that. I don't want to carry any guilty conscience. You heard me?"

"Very sorry Mrs. Vice President."

"So, what happened Professor?"

"Banker on top of a shopping mall."

"Damn! OK now I understand. So how far with the missing subject? Recovered yet?"

"Up and running I suspected it had overheated. The new generation ones are still dependent on crude oil.

The older ones have adapted and use human oil. Once the new ones have absorbed crude oil through their skin, it incapacitates them."
The world war began between the swarm of aliens in the form of boys and humans. Most of the countries woke up to find that their weaponry bases had been destroyed. This was a shock that sends feelings of fear and desolation. After their weaponry was destroyed the inhabitants of several countries woke up to find their skies dark filled with the swarm of the alien boys. This was the most terrifying thing they have ever witnessed. The boys kept circulating the skies. The soldiers gathered outside waiting for the aliens' next move. They had seen what they can do, and the feeling was that of respect. All the other people remained in doors watching the events as they unfold on the televisions. As the soldiers gathered outside, the swarm of aliens in lighting speeds flew down and grabbed whoever they can and disappeared. One after the other and after that they disappeared for days leaving the army waiting for them but above all scared to death. Most kept flicking their heads looking into the skies at any slightest shadow and any real bird's activity in the skies. A Touchladybirdlucky news channel van traveled where the soldiers had temporary settled interviewing the soldiers to gage moral.
"So, what do you make of all this? Do you think they might come back again?"
Questioned the anchor-woman.
"Come back or not this won't change anything. We are prepared to fight until the end. This is our country which we shall defend at any cost."
"Even if it means dying here on the battlefields?"

Queried the anchor-woman.

"Yes. They can't come here and think that they can take what they want from us. This is our country and we shall defend it."

"It seemed that the aliens had dispersed or gone completely. For the first-time in three days the skies are clear as you can see. The aliens that had gathered in the skies have dispersed. Where they have gone, no one knows. Are they going to come back again? Could be yes could be no. No one knows for sure. Many have dreaded the confrontation in the wake of events in the neighboring country where all the soldiers that had gathered were killed. Annie reporting for Touchladybirdlucky news."

The aliens for the next days were very busy carrying oil both the new ones and the old ones. At a military base in one of the countries fighter jet planes are sent to search for these aliens. For days, they could not find them. They looked at the satellite but still they could not locate them. Why? No one knows some suggested that they might have gone on invisible mode.

"Sir, we can't seem to locate the aliens we have searched all over in the air it seems either they are not on land or have gone in hiding."

"Why would the aliens visit us and why are they taking the dead people and where to? This is very strange."

"Do you think they might come back?"

"Yes. They lingered in the air for three days that means they didn't get what they are after. If they had disappeared the first day I was going to say maybe they got what they wanted. I am not sure they got what they wanted. They are playing games I think

they want to ambush us."
Everywhere else things have just started going back to normal. People had started going back to work. Everyone was rebuilding hoping for a good future. Days later the army was still stationed in the fields near the coast. People were more relaxed than the previously days. It was a sunny afternoon when there was a huge buzzing sound of voices in the air. The soldiers were sitting down relaxing after stressful days of just standing and waiting. A swarm of alien boys this time even more in numbers flew down in lightning speeds spraying everyone and every vehicle in the field repeatedly but all in a matter of seconds. Soon after people and vehicles were all engulfed in flames. People were burning alive. Noises of screaming and crying was that deafening that it was sickening. Those who tried to escape were shot dead. In a matter of seconds the whole place was in flames. Other soldiers were rolling on the ground trying to put out the flames buy sadly they were sprayed again and again. The television crew was also burned to death. The world trembled with fear and locked themselves inside their houses and some headed for the airports. This was like the end of the world. The aliens were going to occupy the land themselves. Weeks later. The President and the Vice President are at a ceremonial re- opening of the gun making plant. A large crowd had gathered outside. "Ladies and gentlemen these are tough times. I believe you all have seen what is happening all over the world. The world is under attack by the aliens. Today I took this decision to start arms production in the hope that tomorrow we might need them. The world has changed. We must be prepared. We humans shall be

one. We shall fight this war together." Everyone cheered and applauded. What was happening worldwide was beyond belief? It took hundreds of years to build a nation that was destroyed in seconds. "Mr. President in case that we are attacked are we in a position that we will be able to defend ourselves?" "We will do our best as a nation. We are stronger and the chances of us being attacked are slim. We will remain vigilant though and these weapons might help us defend our nation, defend our rights in the future." "Are we not supposed to be emphasizing aerial fleet since these aliens spend most of the time in the air rather than making more guns?"

"We have enough aerial support now and we will continue to make more and you have seen that it might be useless against these alien. Our initial thought is that they sent a small team first to explore and clean the area first before they bring everyone." Later the President was talking to the Vice President outside near the garden.

"Mr. President that was an excellent speech. These are tough times we have to be prepared."

"Thank you, Mrs. Vice President, I hope everything will be OK in the end."

"Fingers crossed."

CHAPTER NINE

Alvis had worked for the military for some years now. After finishing his training, he had been given a post at the headquarters. After noticing the recent strange activities, he had volunteered to visit the place and find out for himself. He was nervous though. He had seen on the television how they destroyed two nations in seconds. If nothing is done, he was afraid that his country would be the next to be attacked. He arrived in the area near the coast and camped. He waited for it to get dark before he put surveillance. Night time arrived, and he wore appropriate gear and ventured outside. The night was lovely with a cool breeze but was dark though. He arrived near the coast the main area were there has been major activities. He scanned the area and looked around. There were no major activities for some time. He swam in the coastal waters. He heard some noises in the air and looked upward. It seemed that there were birds up in the sky. He swam away from underneath these birds quietly afraid of being seen. Suddenly the swarm flew down swiftly and every one of them submerged in the water. The scene was shocking. It was like the birds' fish feasting scene where all the birds would circle above the water targeting the fish underneath and with swift speeds all shoot into the water. Alvis ducked and swam away from the aliens. The splashing noises were so loud that Alvis knew that these were no mere birds. There was more to it. He raised his head and waited. The birds disappeared for a while. It was minutes later that they all rose in the sky. He looked at them as they rose upward. For the first-time, he saw what he was dealing with. Somehow it was a relief to know that they were in the form of boys, at least humans, he had expected to see some ugly faced-scary aliens. He just found it hard to believe that they were aliens. Initially, it was like watching the kids play and squabble over a football or something like that, until the aliens started fighting and pushing each other. He was gob smacked when one flipped upward and vertical floating in the air upside down. Instantly another one grabbed it and they fell in the water fighting with at extreme speeds sending a huge splash all over drenching and sinking Alvis from his hiding place. The whole group flew up and then down straight shooting into the water with tremendous speeds. They all rose from the water pushing the two fighters out of the water into mid-air. They hovered and circled the fighters and watched then fight. After a while the fighters emerged again in the water. One alien boy flew out of the water and up above into the skies at the same time and as one plunged into the water. This time when the two fighters flew out of the water the group fights them.

Then only one of them then flew up all the way to the skies and stayed there for a while. Whoever beat the rest and escapes from the water can go higher up. After a long fight and squabbling another alien boy rose to the sky. The two then flew very fast and shoots into the water. The rest then formed a circle around them. After that then they flew away. Alvis shocked hid and waited. He regretted getting into the water as he had no camera to take any pictures. Had he stayed near his camp site he could have captured the world's first glimpse of the aliens. He realized that it might be difficult to catch any as they were always together. He knew one way was to shoot one of them. He needed proof, back home he will be a national hero. Just imaging killing one of these things that had terrorized mankind, surely that will be something. He quickly left the coastal waters and went back to his camp site. He didn't waste time, he took his small bag and checked his gun, then binoculars and a camera. The aliens after leaving the waters started carrying oil. They had increased the speed thereby reducing the time it took to transport the oil. The Professor is in his office with Angela one of the scientists and the software engineer.

"Strange behavior if you ask me. Have you seen the recent footage? Look how they are fighting. They are robots for Christ's sake."

"Let me see."

"I don't understand why do robots fight each other? Do they feel?"

"These are astonishing ones but for those fighting each other they are the first to be introduced. It seemed over the months they have evolved. Initially they used to feed on crude oil. Months later I was shocked that they were using human oil. For some reason, unknown to us they have highly developed. They fight for positions and ranks. Deliberately, they disobey some commands that conflict with their judgment."

"Really? What I don't understand is that why the first generation is smarter than the last generation?"

"Normally if it's just a robot yes. These somehow have gained experienced and a better understand of things probably that's why."

"Wait Professor rewind that video I thought I have seen someone."

The Professor rewound the video, and they both looked at the footage attentively.

"There! There! Look! Who is that?" Queried Angela.

"Oh, my, my, what do we have here? I have to talk to the Vice President straight away."

The Vice President was in her house when the phone rang.

"Yes, speaking."

"We need to talk." Alvis walked back to the coastline this time with his gear, a gun, a binocular and a camera. He sat in his hiding place and waited. Tiredness caught up with him that when he covered his head with the hood hat, he started dosing off. For some minutes, he slept. It was the sound of the splashing alien boy that woke him up. He looked and saw one of them in the water before the boy disappeared deep under the water. Minutes later the boy came out of the water and flew instantly. He aimed the gun, but it was too late to shoot the had already disappeared. He waited and before he knew it another one arrived and straight dived into the water. He aimed and waited patiently. This one took too long underneath and before it came out another one arrived. Alvis aimed at the new arrival but it suddenly disappeared into the water. Instantly the other one resurfaced and flew into the air at tremendous speeds. Alvis smiled. These aliens where interchanging. This time he edged forward and aimed. As soon as the other one popped out he took it out unhesitatingly. One bullet and the alien is in the water. He smiled and quickly entered the water looking for the alien. He searched for some time and found the alien laying some distance away from the shooting point. He dragged it out of the water. He carried it to his camping site. He took pictures and tried to communicate with it. He noticed a familiar smell. He touched the robot everywhere and realized that it was bleeding oil. He realized that it had crude oil in its system.

"Man made? Causing that havoc who is behind this?" Shocked and upset Alvis looked at the alien robot. Alvis heard a large buzzing noise coming from the waters. The noise soon died then he heard a buzzing sound outside his tent. He picked up his gun and aimed in every direction flipping his head left and right. His tent is ripped from the ground upward leaving him exposed. A boy stood vertical upside down above him. He looked up in the sky and saw the other boys circling him. He threw the gun away and imitated the alien boy he had shot. He lay down in the same position. The other boy hovering above him slowly flew down. The robot poured oil down covering Alvis and the injured robot. Alvis remembered how they had set everyone on fire. Instincts kicked in, he got up and ran for his life. The chase began, one on one. The others remained hovering in the air behind. Alvis being a soldier had advantages. He ducked down and quickly turned looking backward and fired three consecutively shots narrowly missing the alien boy. The alien boy flipped backward, to the side before disappearing up into the sky dodging the consecutive shots fired by Alvis. This was his trade mark, marksman-kill-shots that had earned decorations for Alvis in the army years ago. He had met his match. In three consequent and linked moves the alien had ducked all bullets. Shocked and surprised Alvis knew he had no chance. The alien then instantly drops down with frightening speed before touching Alvis' shoulder. Alvis screamed rubbing his shoulder as he was nearly burnt.

"What are you trying to do? Cook me alive Ha?" Screamed Alvis. He rolled on the ground and got up again and ran for his life. He looked backward looking for the boy alien but he was not there. Swiftly he got punched in the chest and staggered backward and instantly the boy touched his body sending his temperature soaring. He pulled a knife and tried to stab the alien but instantly the alien flipped upward and hovered in the skies before instantly in a blink of an eye carried Alvis up in the air before letting him fly. Unfortunately, gravity beats him and Alvis dropped down. Somehow this soldier wasn't finished. It was not over yet. He got a gun from his back as he was falling and fired a shot hitting the alien and instantly the alien dropped down onto him crashing him to the ground. The other aliens arrived to find one of them injured and besides Alvis but already draining succulent oils from his fried body. The alien shoulder had oils coming out. But his wound had begun the healing process. They circled around him and all of them touched Alvis taking some oils. After draining Alvis, they carried one of their own, the injured one to the coastal waters and placed him inside. A car is on the road coming from the other side. Peter is in the car. He looked in the glove compartment and suddenly an animal appeared in front of the car with what looked like a human hand. Peter slammed on the brakes. He got out of the car and looked around. He walked to what looked like a half-eaten human body. Next to the man was a camera and on the other side a gun. He picked up both and returned to the car. He drove off. The aliens looked for the other injured alien and placed him in the water. The next day they were both okay healed and flying again. A man in a hurry knocked the office and entered quickly. There is a man sitting on the desk. He is the general manager of the oil refinery. "Sir nearly all our oil is gone."

"Don't be daft that can't be possible. It will require years for someone to extract all that oil."

"Look at today's readings?"

Raul showed the manager the charts and reports. The manager looked confused and surprised.

"It could be that the meters have malfunctioned mind you these meters are nearly ten years old." Somewhere in the suburbs a 4x4 car parked outside and two men dressed in military uniform got out of the car. They entered one of the houses and knocked at the door. A young girl rushed to the door and opened the door.

"Daddy! Daddy! Your friends are here."

"I will be down in a minute."

"Tell mum I am going, I see you tonight."

The three men entered the car, and the car drove off.

"I want an update. Is there any new information?"
"We have some evidence we believe might be helpful. Some photos and a gun has been found and it might just point us in the right direction."
One of the man, Tom handed the photos.
"Is that a boy?" asked Chuck.
"At first, we thought so, but look at his shoulder."
"What do you think this is?"
"If you are shot Sir, you will bleed blood and not some black oily fluid."
"Ah, you are right. I haven't looked at that properly. What kind of alien is this? Bird like a real boy."
"Might have imitated a young boy."
"Photos could be fake."
"We thought that, but this person gave us the coordinates and that's where we are going now. It is a bit long drive though, but we will get there, eventually."
On arrival, they looked for the place it was later that they found the place and the partly eaten body still there.
"The place in the picture isn't here we need to see that place first. Later they found the place, and they collected soil samples and looked around for any evidence. They noticed that the place was close to the coast. They traveled to the coastline and searched the whole area. They found split crude oils in the water. It was later that they found two skeletons and on close examination they turned out to be that of a female and a man. Luckily nearby they uncovered a wallet partly covered underneath with IDs. In the afternoon Chuck is research about the person whose IDs they had found at the coast.
"Strangely this is a missing person."

"Find out if he had a son and a wife."

"Yes. He had a son and a wife who disappeared at the same time. But another article says that the boy was later found. The boy suits the description as well."

"Maybe you should find out first he could be the boy who was maybe later returned."

"I will be on my way there."

The next day Chuck was outside a house that used to belong to Luke, Hailey and their son Gregor. The house had new owners living there now. He learned of the death of Hailey's sister and her boyfriend. He heard the neighbor's stories that Gregor returned at one point and that at some time after that he had visited his friend. He was given the address and he drove there.

"So, are you sure that Gregor once came here after he was reported missing?

"Yes, we found him lying down in the kitchen but subsequently left the next day."

"Was he the same person, or he had changed?"

"When he came back he didn't talk much, he was very quiet."

"Did he do anything strange? How did you find him?"

"He was on the floor. He wanted oil, we took him upstairs and placed him in the tub."

"Oil? Was it to drink?"

"No for all over his body he was very hot."

Chuck for the following weeks he had been going to the coastline where Luke and his family died. He searched the coastline for clues. It was later that he started to notice a pattern. He looked all over the coastal area and found out that there was oil in the water at most of the times. Maybe this is the sole reason why the alien boys came this side. The pictured boy had exactly this kind of oil, dark and very viscous. The test results showed that it was indeed crude oil. So maybe the boy was in the water in the first place. He parked his car nearby and waited. One day he found one of the boys in the water unable to move. He was very unresponsive but wide awake. He bundled him in the car and drove off. He took the boy to the nearest military barracks. They carried him inside. There were monitors that were switched on and computers. They locked him in a private room and observed him from outside. While he was inside Chuck heard the commotion outside. There were noises and people were running around. Chuck looked outside and saw soldiers running. He went outside to find out. The sky was dark with aliens. It was unbelievable. Fear crippled him. The general approached him.

"I told you not to bring him here? I said take him home with you."

"But Sir I have a family and a young kid."

"I have all these men to protect and look after. Look in the sky. Once they start pissing oil, then that's it. Honestly, I don't want that today."

"I can still go with him to my place I need decoy but you might be at risk if they know he is no longer here they might attack you."

"What's wrong with him? Did you shoot him?"

"No I found him just like that. Something to do with the oil. He was overheating I guess."

"Are you sure this is an alien?"

"Can't tell, could be could be not."

"So, what is your plan? Can I take him or not?" I guess you might as well leave him here we will observe him probably you are right they might not attack us. Unexpectedly the aliens started flying on top of the building in which the other boy was in. They floated in the air upside down and looked inside just before they disappeared. Soon half of the aliens disappeared. After a while the alien boy started feeling hot. He started shaking very hard.

"Something is wrong. Open. Right now, He is boiling."

"We can't do that. What if he attacks us?"

"If he wanted to attack, he could have attacked us. I brought him. I will take him away."

"Where has his friends gone to? Are you sure they haven't gone to collect oil to drench us?"

"Supposed so. That's why I am saying I should take him home with me."

"Is it raining what is that noise?"

The general and Chuck ran outside and saw their worst fears manifested. The aliens were about to attack. A siren went off that caused panic among the aliens as well and soon they descended with lightning speeds pouring oil on top of the buildings and everyone. Another half just behind them hovering in the air soaking everyone and everything. Instantly the whole place was ablaze. The captured alien's temperature kept rising very high and steam started coming out. Slowly the alien started to move and oil started leaking out from its body. After a while the alien gained consciousness and sat up. Instantly it turned into a small super jet and rocketed through the ceiling. Chuck looked in astonishment. Soon it disappeared. The soldiers fought hard managing to shoot some but as they fall to the ground, the other aliens would instantly come and pick them and take them to the ocean and dropped them there. All the soldiers who had died were taken away as well. No dead people were left after the fighting. Chuck and the general escaped as soon as the captured alien escaped.

"General I have an idea. We can fight back."

"What do you have in mind Chuck?"

"Not sure if this can work but they use oil on us so why can't we use oil on them."

"What are you talking about?"

"I think I know why the alien was incapacitated. It absorbed oils. Crude oil to be precisely. It is allergic to this kind of oil. It makes sense now. I checked the waters where I found him incapacitated, there is crude oil everywhere. So, if we use bullets or oil sprays maybe we can catch and destroy these. Normal bullets seem not to work."

"OK, we try that I need to gathered some fighters first all my men were cooked alive. That's just horrific to watch. What I don't understand is that why they take them after that. Some might have still been alive. Are you telling me that they eat humans too?"

"Why they use fire all the time. Did you see the other alien it heated up first? So, I think they drain human oils. Damn! We are heading for extinction. We are like a food source now."

"Are you saying they are changing from crude oil to human oil?"

"That could explain the relentless. It's not just killing its harvesting. They have never left a human body before. Where do they take these bodies to?"

"Oh, my God! Humans are finished. I think we should follow them somehow. My idea was to tag one of them."

"Very unlucky we had captured one of them. That could have been something."
"Shocked and surprised did you see how it escaped like a spaceship. The speed I just can't believe it." Days after, Chuck arrived home to find the front door opened. Shocked and afraid he entered the living room and found his wife passing food to five boys. His daughter was on the floor playing with these boys. They all looked like the aliens he had seen before. As soon as he had entered the living room, he panicked and shouted.
"Lily come here right now. Who are these people? What do they want? Who invited them?"
"Darling relax, I invited them in. I saw them playing outside. The other one was on top of the roof. Trust me, they speak English. They are not aliens."
"How come they all look alike and wear the same clothes."
"Darling I asked them they said to scare people. A hoax, see nothing to worry about, right boys?"
"Correct, madam." Chuck moved around touching them one by one checking their body temperatures. Four of the five were okay the fifth one was a bit shaking and his body temperature was a bit raised. Chuck looked scared a bit.
"Darling what is it now? I thought we talked about this why you keep on checking. You are scaring them now." Chuck realized that he might be intimidating them so he left and went to his garage. He had brought some oil from the coastline. He took some of the oil and took it to the living room. He entered the living and everyone was there. He had changed into his boxer shorts and he sat down. He watched as they play. After a while he started shaking. He looked at

his wife.

"It's okay don't ask."

After shaking for a while he lay down on the floor and poured oil on the floor and lay down there for a while. The boy who was heating up flipped upward upside down vertical and hovered in the air before landing next to Chuck. Chuck waited for the others but they just looked at each other and stared at his daughter and wife. Chuck realized that the other four were dangerous. The others were eyeing his family. He got up and left the other boy absorbing the oil. He took the oils and walked past the other boys and intentionally poured oil on them. They all quickly rubbed off and removed the oil. Lily got up and went near the boys and they all looked at her hands and legs. One of the boys started sniffing Lily's hands.

"Stop it hold it. What are you doing?"

"Smell good. Smell good."

"Darling take Lily and go to the kitchen. Now."

Sobia took Lily, and they entered the kitchen. Instantly, all the boys floated in the air upside down and circled Chuck. "Run to the car."

"Oil, you, nice oil," remarked one of the boys. The struggle begun and Chuck frequently touched the oil and tried to rub it on them but each time they would float away from him. Sobia started the car and waited for Chuck. Chuck let out the loudest scream before being dragged in the air by his head. The aliens took him outside and swiftly in the air before dropping him down. He dropped onto the bonnet of the car. He raised his bloodied head, he turned around and looked at his wife and daughter with a blooded face and he died. Sobia drove the car away from their home. The four boys after draining Chuck's oils went back in the house and touched the remaining boy who was still laying on the floor. His body temperature had started rising. The four boys went after Sobia and Lily. They caught up with them. Sobia tried to run over one of the boys losing control and the car skidded before stopping facing the way it came. The boys dragged Sobia and Lily out of the car. They were about to fry them when the other boy arrived and a fight broke out. The other boy turned out to be JT the alien. He fought hard to save Sobia and her daughter. Whenever the others tried to take them, he would defend them. The other boys finally gave up. They left them alone. Sobia and Lily and JT entered the car and drove away. The boys flew for a while before all touched the car carrying Sobia, Lily and JT. Sobia and Lily were fried to death by the temperatures. JT kept shaking burning out that in the end he needed oil. At last he touched Sobia and Lily dead bodies and slowly drained their oils. The other boys stood looking at the car with JT, waiting for him to come out. After a while JT came out and fell to the ground shaking. They carried him higher up in the skies and left.

CHAPTER TEN

The President is in his office when someone knocked the door.

"Come in."

The President Mr. Plintz of the neighboring country had secretly visited the President. "What a pleasant surprise. What brings you here my friend?"

"Long story. As you know we are under attack. We have been singled out. The past months were a living horror non-stop constant attack. If it keeps going on like this, we will lose this war against the aliens. In a war like this we are all one. We should be supporting each other. Aliens are ruthless, no feelings whatsoever."

"It's a pity I understand and I honestly sympathize with you. I wish I can help. What do you have in mind.?"

"Now I understand why the aliens attacked us. It never occurred to me but now I think I understand."

"What do you mean my friend?"

"It's a strategic attack. These aliens are much clever than I thought. They attacked us because of the oil."
"What just because you have the oil. Are you sure about that?"
"The funny thing is that they attacked us and used our own oil to roast us so that they can take us and eat us."
"What are you saying?"
"They are cooking us alive and then take everyone with them."
"Do aliens eat people? Don't get me scared like that."
"It's true. I don't understand why they are taking all the people but it's a gruesome thought. Our oil is nearly gone. They used it as food or fuel? We checked our reserves. In just a year they nearly emptied all our reserves." The President sat in his chair and took a long breath.
"Now you see why I came for help. I need oil soon before my country stood still. I don't know what to do. The attacks are now not as bad as the days we hard loads of oil. What do you say my friend?" "I thought you are after guns. Oil? I guess I must come back to you on that one."
"I might get guns as well. I am scared once our oil runs out they might want to wipe us out."
"Today we can make a gun deal tomorrow I will let you know about the oil deal. OK."
The Vice President got up and walked to the window in his office. He stood there for a while and remembered the day he jumped with fear after seeing that small boy.
"What is the Vice President up to? Some women are robust as rocks surely, I surrender with this one. What is she up to now? I just can't seem to understand her?

Why she sent that boy that day? Was she passing a
message or what. Oil? All that oil? Where would she
put all that oil? I wonder?"
These are the questions that were running in the
President's head before he heard a knock on the door.
"Come on in please."
"Mr. President your limousine is ready."
"Thank you I will be there in a minute." The
President left his office and entered his limousine
going out of town. For the first-time fear struck him.
The Vice President had become a formidable force to
be bargained with. What stopping her using these
aliens to over throw him? If she can bring a country
to its knees in a year what about him? Later the
President entered the water processing plant's offices.
"The place is very gigantic. It's scary just looking at
how big this place is."
"Yes, Mr. President, the place is huge recently
completed."
"Correct me if I am wrong. This is a water energy
plant, right?"
"As far as I know yes, Mr. President. What makes you
ask that question?
"I can't remember correctly but I think someone
mentioned oil to me?"
"No not oil I don't think so. Anywhere we will find
out soon. Its opening next month If I am correct. A
couple of weeks ago, though, they delivered oil here I
understand the driver was sent back." The President
looked at the picture of the Vice President on the
wall. He smiled and saluted her before leaving. Later
that week the President was at the conference of all
neighboring Presidents.
"Ladies and gentlemen, we are at a losing war. The

problem is much deeper than we thought. These aliens are too clever for us. They have wiped out all our oil reserves just a year on and we are down on our knees. They ate all my best soldiers."

"The story is the same everywhere. But all I can say is that let's stick together. Let us share resources and ideas. If we try to be selfish, we will all perish. These are real life challenges."

"We borrowed a lot of money against this oil and now it's all gone I just don't know where to start. How are we going to repay all the loans?"

"The only money left is money for defense which we have never cut. Most of our people had gone abroad I can't see how we can survive a year or so in these circumstances."

"The only help I can offer are weapons. After the initial attacks of our neighbors we embarked on a massive production of ammunition. Today we stand to be the world's weapons manufacturer, guns, jet fighters you name it. Maybe not being attacked has something to do with this."

Announced the President. They all looked at him and later offered to have weapons deals as well. Later that day the President was talking with the Chief of National Security.

"It is strange I went to this meeting not knowing what to expect and guess what?"

"What Mr. President."

"I sold a $ billion worth of weapons just like that."

"I think sometimes it's good to be the President." The President smiled, and the limousine cruised back to the city center. The Professor had just rung the Vice President and they are talking on the phone.

"Professor I understand there has been a lot of

incidents exposing our project. Did you send the cleaners?"

"I sent cleaners everywhere apart from the general. He ran, so I guess he still wants to live I thought of maybe contacting him and see if he can take our deal after the country has crumpled?"

"What do you have in mind?"

"I was just thinking that when all this is over who will represent you in all these countries. You won't be able to rule all."

"Professor phase 10 is maybe five to ten years from now." "I think one or two if you want to."

"How can I do that Professor in such a short notice?"

"So many things. The choice is yours. First increase their sense of security by supplying all the weapons they need and you take the valuable money. Today they are stronger but tomorrow people will want food and oil and not weapons. As far as I know this stage has already happened."

"I guess so we need to push very hard and sell more weapons before the aliens stops."

"The options are endless we can spend the whole day talking about this. Back to your question."

The President was in his office weeks later after the weapons deals. He was watching the news channels.

"With sad regrets, we have learned of the death of President Plintz as we have just heard the alien threat has shaken a lot of people and took away any hope people had and this included the President who we understand shot himself in his office. People are saying he was going to be removed, anyway by the people as the country succumbed to its knees. Either way such a loss at these tough times is hard to bear. Mary the news reporter, reporting for

Touchladybirdlucky news."
"Damn I can't believe he is gone. Just last week another President gone. What's happening?"
Quizzed the President. He got up and waked to the cabinet display and poured a glass of wine.
"It's the President can you get my limousine ready."
Later the President was at the Vice President's offices. He knocked the Vice President's office door, but she was not in. He made his way to the basement in the same building straight to the Professor's lab. The Professor was in the lab the door of the lab was open slightly. The Professor was expecting the Vice President it seems. The President entered the lab without saying anything. The Professor was watching one of the footage he had just downloaded. The Professor did not look to see who it was who had just entered the lab. He assumed it was the Vice President.
"Yes, Mrs. Vice President the footage of the President's last minutes on earth."
The President shocked and flabbergasted and frightened too looked closely at the footage. In the footage, President Plintz is holding a gun to his head he looked scared. He tried to talk something, but he put the gun in his mouth. He pulled the trigger and to his relief and shock at the same time. There were no bullets, a kid's hand offered him another gun. He pulled the trigger and blood is seen all over the place. Seconds later the President saw the movement of the camera as if the person who filmed the video was upside down.
"Rewind that I want to see that who was the boy. Show me."
The Professor jumped shock and frightened to find out that it was the President.

"Mr. President, I am afraid this is classified."

"Rewind the clip or else."

"Or else what Mr. President?"

Questioned the Vice President entering the lab. "What is going on? Are you behind all this too? I have seen a little boy in that video. I recognized that boy. I want to see that footage now."

"OK. Professor," ordered the Vice President. They watched the video clip and when the boy's face was in the frame, the Professor paused the video.

"That's the boy who was outside my window. Right?" Queried the President with his eyes wide open.

"Mr. President."

"Just answer me?"

"Yes, that's his job."

"Did you send him to me that day?"

"Professor leave us."

The Professor walked out closing the door behind him.

"It's a program that is written to listen to you. It does what you want. If that is what you want the program helps you achieve that. If you say you want to die today, the program helps you do that."

"How will that kid know if I want to die or not?"

"Don't be upset, you are here because you chose to live. The program listens to your heart. Your heart beat everything and calculate the chances of say taking action A versus action B."

"What are you saying? This boy knows what I want? That's absurd. You have started murdering people? This is just an excuse. Right?"

"I can't say that. I can only tell you that the program is there to give you a way out."

"Is there something I don't know Mrs. Vice

President?"

"OK. I remembered you asking me about the plan and the vision of this project. I will tell you today. I had a vision when I was a kid. In fact, we had a bet. This guy came to me and said I don't think the world will ever be ruled by a woman. Ever since I have developed and redrawn plans. Today I can say that this world as it will come clear to everyone will be mine and all be ruled by a woman."

"Yes, go on."

"I wanted you in my world Mr. President but I think we will have issues in the future."

"Why is that?"

"Remember the oil deal?"

"Yes. Sorry I went and made the deal anywhere."

"Despite my warnings and objections that the deal was not for us you went to make the deal. Just today they phoned me, they said you tricked them since the aliens stole their oil you will steal be abode by this deal. Losing us money. Just today they were asking for cash but I sent them a boy to play with."

"You can't do that? How many do you have to kill?"

"Your choice Mr. President pay-up or I give them a present?"

"OK, go on."

"That blunder nearly cost me a lot of money?"

"What do you mean?"

"We will ever be indebted to them something I didn't want. Soon we will be the richest nation on planet earth. People will come to this country bringing riches with them. No other country on earth shall have oil cars apart from this country. They can have solar cars and electrical cars who cares. But those who want to drive an oil car, petrol or diesel they should come and

stay in this country., for only us will have the oil."
"Why only us? So, many countries have oil."
"Not from end of this year fingers crossed. All that oil has been stolen by aliens."
"It's you Mrs. Vice President. Damn! Where do you get all these ideas from?"
"Can I go on?"
"Yes, go on, Mrs. Vice President."
"When we are the superpower only us will have the capabilities and resources to make weapons, drive cars and fly planes. Only us will have the oil. Only us will fly the planes. And we will buy off other governments and take over. The whole region, if not the whole earth will be mine, or ours if you agree to my demands."
"Agree to what demands?"
"Let me finish first. We will provide the best resources and infrastructure and everything. But this will not come cheaper. See we will form the $50 000 club. You pay us $50 000 and we provide you with everything basic like jobs, a mortgage, insurance, a wife, a car, a dog, I mean everything, if you want a small boy we provide one too. Once you are here, you will work very hard or smarter and help rebuild this country. This is the $50 000 club. It's fair to those with dreams. Now back to your question."
"The project is mine. I understand that you would love to remain the President but you expressed poor judgment and mistrust, regarding the oil deal and above all you completed the deal behind my back. OK it's in the past, for the future you can remain the President but I have the final decision. You spearhead weapons sales I concentrate on oil and the development of this country. What do you say

partner?" Questioned Mrs. Vice President.

"Just one question that's been nagging me; why did you send that boy?"

"A gift. Your friend. I always see you looking outside that window. I gave you something to look at. Shall we Mr. President."

"After you Mrs. Vice President."

CHAPTER ELEVEN

The Vice President and the President are in the limousine going to a ball function. They are all dressed to kill. They are talking and watching what is happening worldwide.

"All the people are rioting and disgruntled. We should be lucky."

"Thanks to you Mrs. Vice President. Look how the rich countries have collapsed within a year."

"In every country people are fighting their governments they have spent money on weapons and now they have no oil and the aliens have deserted them. The pressing issues now are food and oil. Who are they going to turn to Mr. President?"

"God, I guess?"

"Incorrect, my boys. Opening new markets. Everything is going per the plan. We must formally announce the presence of weapons and oil deals as soon as all the governments have been removed and replaced. It took a lot of planning to come to this stage but once you are at this stage, it is a free fall like a jigsaw puzzle. Everything just fit in place." The limousine stopped at the traffic lights. The President looked outside. There were a lot of people outside. It was the most beautiful, peaceful, and lovely scene unlike abroad with scenes of violence and struggling all the time. The past months the President and the Vice President have spent a great deal of time monitoring world events. That was monotonous and depressing, they both felt relieved that they were going to such a pleasant occasion. They arrived and got off the limousine. They were greeted by flashing images. A lot of reporters and photographers had gathered. The last months' press headlines were about war and violence abroad and for a change they were going to report about something nice and pleasant. At the dinner ball, they enjoyed the meal and spoke to a lot of people. It was later that evening when a man was forbidden entry because he was accusing the President of owing his country some oil money. The security guards were quick to come to the rescue. Later somehow the man returned in different clothes disguising himself and he later pulled the trigger. Women screamed when they heard the gunshot sound. No one really knew what was going on. The President opened his eyes and touched himself. He looked next to him and saw a boy laying there looking at him emotionless. He touched the boy and looked at his hands covered in blood. He got up and looked at the man who had shot him. He was down with a bullet in his head. The President shouted for help. "Get this man to the hospital now. A man is down call for help now."

The Vice President looked at the President and smiled without saying anything.

"Who was he? Is he my boy?"

"You can say that Mr. President."

"He served my life today. I am very grateful to you Mrs. Vice President. We are a team now cover my back I cover yours."

He paused and continued talking.

"One question why the blood?"

"An upgrade phase 10 model invisible until when needed."

"Phase 10 already I thought you said this was five to ten years away?"

"On my own Yes, but with my partner one to two."

"You are something Mrs. Vice President."

Miles away a man had just paid the $50 000 club fee and boarded a plane. He looked outside the window and saw the beautiful clouds unlike the memories of yesterday. Yesterday's life was traumatic. He is even scared to sleep in case he is burnt alive. The harsh thing is that yesterday is interwoven with both good memories and bad memories. A country he loved had been made desolate. A country he fought for had been torn apart and vandalized. A place he used to call home is no longer home. Just a shadow of yesterday. A new country new hope and greater dreams to dream about. Better life and a new challenge. Constantly he looked up in the skies. He still sees all the pain of yesterday. Sometimes as a reflex he ducks even at the slightest movement in the air. The aliens had tormented him. He saw all his man burn in the fire. It was horrific and memories still lingered on. It was the sweet voice of the air hostess that woke him up from this nightmare.

"Any drinks?"

"Just a soda. If you don't mind."

For a while he looked at the air hostess. She made him think about his girlfriend. Not because she looked like her no, they were totally different. It's the look in her eyes. He remembered how he had met his girlfriend. That was such a good time and the day he left her standing outside his house. He also remembered the day he returned to find the house empty. A man stood up in the front seat of the plane and when he saw him he felt depressed and felt like dying. The man reminded him of his friend whom he could not save. It was such a long time, but it felt like yesterday. War destroyed everything good but who should have guessed this was a war of its kind. Fighting the fastest enemy, he had ever fought, very small but ferocious. They have been defeated in seconds. Just to imagine that they spent days preparing for a war that lasted seconds. He still smelt the bodies of his friends who burned to death. He still remembered how they were taken. He felt his stomach turning. That is very frightening just to know that you are going to be killed and be eaten. What on earth was going? Why his country? On arrival Quinton checked-in a hotel and proceeded to the city center. Later he entered a government building and made his way up. A woman came off the lift and went downstairs. He entered the lifts and went upstairs. He came across a reception. He looked around and left the building without saying anything.

"Hello Sir, what is your business here?"

"Who are you? Why are you asking me such a private question? Who wants to know?"

"I would like to know what you are doing in here and when are you planning to go back?"

"Who are you? None of your business."

"I am the new just introduced city security officer. You are my first customer."

"No I am not, find someone else."

"I am not trying to be funny you know but look even my pad is written that you are my first customer." Quinton ignored the man and left. The man looked at him and wrote something down and left. For the coming days, Quinton familiarized himself with the city. He had been to all the places that was in his $50,000 club contract. He registered everywhere. He moved from the hotel and into the city apartment. One morning he took a shower and after the shower he wiped steam off the mirror. He jumped backward. He looked again and touched everywhere but there was no one. He swore to himself that there was someone else in the bathroom. He saw a face that quickly vanished. He thought he saw a boy inside his room who disappeared instantly. He looked everywhere and punched the air. Since this day, he kept looking everywhere. He started feeling like he was being watched. He was going outside one day when he saw the boy in the corridor when he blinked the boy had disappeared. Julia a beautiful lady left her room and was about to close the door when Quinton stopped and looked inside.

"Excuse me that's private property."

"It just depends private to who. Just today after taking a shower I saw a boy in my room and he disappeared instantly. I left the room in the corridor I saw another boy when I was passing him he disappeared."

"You are joking, right? So, let me guess you are checking my room to see if my room has these invisible boys, right? You are something. Please some of us we have work to go to."

"Can I come for a coffee later?

"No stay with the invisible boy."

"Very funny."

Later that day the Professor was in the lab when he had a visitor. "Professor I have a stubborn guy in one of the apartment. I swear at one point steam removed my camouflage, and we looked face to face. I instantly disappeared with invisible mode but trust me you should have seen the look on his face. I still laugh if I think about it."

"What did he do? Is he not cooperating?"

"His days are running out. Time is moving very fast what he doesn't know is that he must do everything on the list in three months to qualify."

"By the way things are going, I think he is planning to stay forever without even qualifying?"

"Maybe he need your magic touch. Push him a bit. I don't want him to jump over the balcony like that crazy girl."

"What's his name?"

"He said that his name is Quinton but when I searched his wallet, he has a military badge. His is called general."

"The general, general."

"How am I supposed to know that?" The next day Julia was in her hotel room and she deliberately let the steam fill the bathroom. After some time, she looked everywhere but did not find the invisible boy. She finished taking a bath and left the apartment but first she went to Quinton's room. She knocked his room, but he was not in. She walked toward her room first. She had just walked past her room when the door to her room opened and closed. She screamed and runaway. Later that day Quinton was in town going to one of his appointments when the city security officer stopped him.

"Hello, we meet again. I have a word of advice for you would you like to watch and visit the best attractions for three months for $50,000?"

"Are you crazy $50,000 for three months? I wouldn't pay anything for that three months.!

"There must be some mistake then."

"What do you mean? Elvis, right?"

"Yes, Mr. Quinton."

"How did you know my name? I did not tell you my name?"

"How did you know my name I did not tell you my name?"

"OK forget about it. Don't follow me."

"But it's my job to tell you this."

"OK tell me and forever don't tell me again."

"Mr. Quinton, you are in the $50,000 club. They don't tell you about this, but within three months you must do everything on the list to qualify to stay enjoying the benefits."

"And if I don't."

"You will lose right to an apartment, everything you have right now. Your $50,000 will expire on the 90th day. You will be destitute and most people in that situation kill themselves and have their parts removed and maybe your body will be fed to the aliens."

"What aliens how did you know that?"

"Mr. Quinton that's not important. If you don't believe me after three months you will experience the worst time of your life. You will start seeing the invisible man. Once that have started then you are finished."

"What do you mean finished? I just got here a few weeks ago, they told me I just pay $50,000 and I stay here forever. Who is the person behind this? Is this a scam?"

"Mrs. Vice President if you have got time I would like to show you something. Can I come to your office later?"

"I am free now come now I will be busy in the afternoon." Later.

"What is it Professor?"

"I think you should see this."

The Vice President and the Professor looked at the video.

"Is that one of us?"

"Correct I was shocked to see that myself."

"What does this mean. Is it evolution?"

"They have a leader now if they don't do what he wants he grounds them. In the footage, he tried to kill the other robot. That's beyond the norm. With every phase the robots are becoming smarter and smarter."

"So, what do we expect in the future? Evolution at its best or what?"

"Correct."

The Vice President is in the conference room with a lot of delegates. They had been talking for some time now. A man hesitantly entered the conference room and looked around. He looked at everyone in the conference room. He looked at the woman and drew his pistol. To his surprise the woman did not even react she just looked at him and stood up.

"Who are you? What do you want?"

"Are you the Vice President? Are you responsible for the $50,000 club? Are you responsible for creating the aliens?

"Mrs. Vice President. Yes. The $50,000 club. Yes, but aliens no."

"This $50,000 club is it fake?"

"It's not fake you just need to read between the lines."

"I paid $50,000 and you say after three months I don't qualify just because I did not do what you requested in three months?

"Yes, something like that."

"Are you telling me that after paying you all that money I am not going to be here forever? Do you know what I went through to gain that money? I fought aliens, I lost friends, relatives and my girlfriend in the fire. They were all cooked alive. I sold my house and together with the insurance money I paid the $50,000 deposit which I understand I will get back at the end. And someone told me that this is a hoax. So, you would rather cheat people, right? But today I will punish you for that for all my soldiers who were cooked alive and eaten by your aliens." Quinton pointed a gun instantly at the Vice President.

"For all my soldiers who died in vain."

Quinton pulled the trigger twice. The Vice President did not panic or show any fear neither did she get shot. She remained standing and pulled a gun herself.

"Let's see if you know this trick."

Quizzed the Vice President pulling the trigger herself twice. Quinton lay in a pool of blood.

"How did you do that?" asked Quinton really surprised looking if his gun had bullets.

"I know that."

Held the Vice President. She flipped her fingers and to Quinton's horror behold the aliens that terrorized his men and girlfriend.

"So, it was you, you steal our oil and our money, so, now you are creaming me to the max you want even the sale of the house proceeds and the insurance as well. Why? Was the oil not enough? So, what were you going to do after three months has expired?"

"What I am going to do now." Replied the Vice President.

"And what's that?"

Inquired Quinton. The Vice President walked to Quinton and stood in front of him.

"General I admire you but you know too much. And to answer your questions I am going to harvest you. Sell all your organs after that whatever is left I will feed to the aliens including all your fluids everything."

"Any more questions general before I finish you off?"

"Do you keep an invisible alien in my apartment?" The Vice President laughed and looked at the general.

"In every house, there is one, I know all what you did since the day you moved in there. Unstoppable have you ever thought about that? A genius plan, a brilliant idea and endless riches."

The general reached for his breast pocket and took out a photo and gave it to the Vice President.

"My girlfriend where is she. Did she die too?"

The Vice President looked at the photo.

"Honestly, I don't know the aliens harvest too. So, they might have taken her."

"They harvest? They harvest what?"

"Evolution general, they harvest human oil, the best oil there is. We started them on crude oil but with time they have jumped to human oil."

"Don't you think that in the future that can be a problem? I am just thinking that what if they started eating people?"

"Our future general, why should you care if you won't be in there. I gave you Julia as your wife if you had listened to the robot you could have earned a lot of points but I am afraid you will never change. Even now you would rather bleed to death than ask for forgiveness and a new start. Good bye general thanks for the $50,000 tip."

"A lot of people sold everything they had houses, cars, insurance policies, to come to the dream land. They paid the $50,000club fee. Stick with the rules and see your money have greater returns or rebel and be harvested or be drained by the aliens."

CHAPTER TWELVE

The aliens spent many years after in the wilderness away from the home country. One day the aliens violated an order. They refused to use crude oil choosing human oil instead. JT together with TK later assumed leadership roles.

"They can't tell us what we should do and what we should not do. After all what are they to us? Nothing than leg-oil. So, why we the superiors should listen to them? We can fly they can't. We don't die they die? We don't get old but they do. I think we are the superior ones so I say we go there and settle there. We should ask them to come over here. We cleaned this place for them. If they refuse, I swear I am going to make hair oil out of them, cook them first," threatened TK.

"TK is right we spent too many years in the wilderness. It's time we change with the humans. They should come this side. We reserved all the oils for them. We have prepared future oil reserves for them."

"What if they fight us? What if they force us to do what they want themselves instead of what we want?" Questioned one of the alien.

"We can't let them force us. We must find a way of knowing what they are thinking. Others we will lose."

"Humans are the weakest creatures. They can't fly anything that does not fly is doomed. If it wasn't for the fresh daily oil requirement, I could have said let's cook all of them today and drain the oil." The Professor promptly ran to the Vice President's office and knocked the door. The Vice President was very busy with investors. Professor you know how I don't to be disturbed when I am with my visitors. The Professor was breathing heavily failing to catch his breath.

"I would not ask if it was important. We have a problem an emergency which I cannot say in front of your delegates."

"OK I will be with you after a while. Make yourself at home."

"Mrs. Vice President that's not what I meant I was talking in the lines of sending them home."

"What is it first?"

"We have a situation the boys have revolted and they are coming here they are asking if we can go and stay there?

"Are you joking since when can they disobey an order?"

"You will be shocked by their demands just wait until they have arrived. I have never expected to hear that. They are threatening as well they said you are just hair oil to them."

"What is our worse scenario? And our best option."

"Worse is if they don't obey forever which means we must do what they want."

"Best option is well they change their minds and go back.".

"In case it turns ugly how many of them can we rely on to be on our side?"

"As far as I know one, JT only unless if he can manage to persuade the others to support him. TK is the main threat. He is the one who is saying that; humans nothing but just hair oil."

"Reprogram all the invisible ones to protection us but remain invisible. Everyone in the city began leaving the city as news of the aliens, invasion spread. The city was always busy and for the first-time it was deserted. People either locked themselves inside or hide in basements. A new era was approaching. Evolution had come so fast than expected. Was there going to be a new world order where the aliens were the superior ones or what? For the few brave ones who had stayed in the streets or watched from the city buildings what was happening was never witnessed before. A wind blows across the street lifting all litter from the street floor and spinning them into the air. A whistling sound is heard from one end to the other. A torn garment from a female's dress rises in the skies and spins several times before it is crashed from one building to the other as it rises above the tall city buildings. Other small plastic papers are raised in the air as well. Rick looked from his apartment window. He looked as the plastics and clothes are lifting higher up. Rick stood at the city apartment window and followed the traveling directional patterns of the plastics and the cloth. He looked up and saw the sky high above filled with small birds circulating like the sea birds just before a great storm. He walked to the couch and sat down next to his girlfriend and touched her tummy. He kissed her tummy and put his head on her lap as she watched the television. In the television, the anchorman is talking, and the pictures being shown are those of the aliens circulating in the skies.

"The city is like a ghost town, deserted totally opposite to what life is like here on normal days. The reason? Visitors from hell as one correctly puts it. The aliens after menacing the neighboring countries have finally reached the dream land the land of milk and honey. It's not a surprise to see the city like this it is believed that our dear friends have developed tests for our juices and one day we might find ourselves on their menu? (pointing to the skies) If you look up there you will find out that those small birds in the sky are indeed our visitors. In the neighboring countries, they have left inhabitable areas miles after miles. The question that is on everyone's mind is why they have come to the city? Finns reporting for Touchladybirdlucky news." The Vice President and the President are in the office talking and watching what was happening with some government ministers and staff. In front of them is a big television flat screen. They are watching the aliens in the air circulating in the skies.

"They are too many if you ask me," declared Marlon.

"For them strength in numbers." Suggested Tim.

"What if they have come just to cook us, drain our fluids and disappear?"

"It's a sickening thought. It feels like the end of the world. I don't understand why they are spending more time in the skies up there. If they really wanted to negotiate, they should have just arrived and talked to us."

"Maybe they are waiting for it to get dark so they can attack us in the dark."

"Mr. President, so, what are your views regarding all this?" Asked a reporter with Touchladybirdlucky news.

"Son, in times like this where we are dealing with such external forces even myself I might not have the correct answers. However, having said that, we are determined to make sure us humans we will be the superior ones. No alien will come here and try to impose rules and try to take our freedom and rights from us."

"Mr. President are we prepared to fight back in case they decided to attack us?"

Questioned the reporter.

"We have weapons to defend ourselves but they might not be ideal weapons against these aliens. Our first option is to listen first. If they offer peace deals, we will take them only if they are beneficial to us."

"Mr. President rumor has it that they burn people alive and take all the oils. Any comments about that.?"

"If they cook me after I have died and eat me I don't see why not, we do the same to animals?" Everyone burst into laughter.

"On a serious note our lives matter and we shall defend our nation and if that means killing all of them then so be it." Later one of the alien flew down and landed in the city. He looked everywhere and flipped upside down vertical with his head down and floated in the air. Those who were in the city looked outside secretly at the alien hovering in the air. The sight of this alien floating in the air sends feelings of fear across the city. The hovering alien circled before flying back in the air. People watched as the alien joined the other liens. Minutes later a swarm of aliens began to descend. Looking from the apartment buildings it was like seeing a swarm of locust descend on a virgin field to wreak havoc. The sky's color changed as the aliens descend. For some they knew hell has break loose. This was like the end of the world. As they descended, they sprayed oil onto the cars parked outside as they descended and set the cars on fire. A huge fire ball is sent into the sky causing all the aliens to retreat and fly back upward. They descended again and this time all circled around TK and JT at the middle. They landed in the streets. On one end the cars are burning and on the other hand the aliens are walking on land but constantly some flipped upward then upside head down. Hovering in the skies. They stopped outside the government office. The Professor is in the lab watching all this on the big screen. A drunkard walked out of one of the streets and staggered toward the alien group.

"You bloody aliens trying to take our city. This is our city and our country so go away." He staggered and stopped he drank from a small bottle that he placed back in his jacket pocket. The leader of the aliens flipped and hovered in the air above now surrounded by the other aliens. He looked at one of the aliens and the alien hovered toward the drunkard upside down. It circled the man for a while. The aliens formed a pyramid shape and TK floated to the top of the pyramid. After a while TK descended and walked to the drunkard and stood next to him he touched the drunkard man and started walking and talking to him.

After a while TK floated back to the top of the pyramid.

"I think it wants to talk to you, and not to the drunkard," suggested one of the members of the staff. The phone rang and the Vice President answered the call.

"Yes, Professor."

"I can go and talk to them and find out what they want?"

"Are you sure you would be safe?"

"I think I will be OK." The Professor appeared outside and walked toward the aliens. The leader of the aliens, TK looked at the Professor and the aliens rearrange the pyramid and stretched it higher. TK floated on top JT underneath him and another alien floated under JT on the third level. This alien, his name was Chad. Chad then floated down and met the Professor they spoke for some time before the Professor went back into the building. He phoned the Vice President.

"He said, they want to talk to the leader I assumed the President."

"Is it safe Professor?"

"I can't tell but sounds hostile. I would send the invisible ones as well just in case."

The Vice President looked at the staff and then at the President.

"They want to talk to you Mr. President." There was silence everyone looked at the President. The President stood up and walked toward the door. The President looked at the Vice President and touched his chest. The Vice President nodded her head. The President walked outside full of confidence. The people who were watching leaned on the windows as the President approached the aliens. He didn't look afraid at all. The aliens stopped and reassembled changing positions on the pyramid. TK remained at the top, JT remained at second position. As the President arrived in front of the alien pyramid. JT floated down from second level to meet the President.

"Wait, a minute."

The President looked back at the building he just came out of. He spoke with JT and started walking backward, and straight into the building. He arrived in the office and looked at everyone a bit embarrassed. "They want the leader of the people, you Mrs. Vice President." In her heart, she smiled this was what she wanted. This was her dream come true. She shook the President's hand and walked outside. As soon as she was outside the aliens started flipping up and down circling TK showing contempt. When she was near them they formed the pyramid again with TK still on top. TK descended from the top and floated toward the Vice President. He landed downward and when they were close, it seemed the alien leader TK knelt in front of the Vice President. He looked like he was struggling and like some people were holding him down. There was commotion as his aliens tried to advance forward but somehow, they seemed to fail. "Let me go who is holding me? Let me go right now?"

"You think you are clever and smarter than all these aliens, right? You cause everyone else to disobey my commands right. I have aliens smarter and more powerful than you. You are a phase one robot after you we have created even more sophisticated ones than you. Now you don't even know who is holding you right? Look."

Explained the Vice President pointing her eyes at her side and flipping her fingers. TK looked on his side and suddenly a scary robot appeared next to him that quickly disappeared in a flash.

"Now you listen to me. I want you to go back and do as you are told okay? Resume oil extraction and transportation and you are not allowed in the city without permission or prior invitation until oil extraction is finished."

The Vice President turned around and went back to the office building. TK is escorted up and to the skies by the invisible aliens. The rest of the group glided up and hovered in the skies. The crowds left the buildings and walked into the streets, cheering and dancing. Later that evening the Vice President is taking with the news reporter.

"So, Mrs. Vice President today you have entered the history books. What did the alien leader say to you? Is our future guaranteed?" Questioned Marta.

"The aliens want us to be under them. They are saying that they are superior to us, they can fly and that we are just hair oil to them.

"What were your feelings going through all that? I know if it was me I might have frozen with fear." The Vice President paused and looked in the camera for a while silent.

"I want all you the inhabitants of this great nation to know that we as a nation we are not going to be intimated and be afraid of these aliens. We must stand together and defend what is rightfully ours."

"Mrs. Vice President is there a chance that this might escalate into a war with the aliens and what words of hope and courage can you give to them."

"Since the day, the aliens invaded the neighboring countries we worked exceptionally hard as your leaders me and the President. We embarked on a multi-billion project. Today I am proud to tell you that what happened today is more than what your eyes saw. I want each one of you to know this. We are prepared to go to war with these aliens. So, don't be afraid we have managed to create a personal body guard for each one of you to protect you from the aliens."

"What do you mean Mrs. Vice President?"

The world was watching and looked and listened attentively. As they were watching the reporter Marta jumped as if someone poked her on her butt. She looked backward and instantly she jumped and touched her backside looking at the Vice President. People who were watching started laughing for a while. The Vice President started laughing as well.

"I apologize Marta but it wasn't me."

"Mrs. Vice President it's only you and me around here and definitely I did not poke myself." "Ladies and gentlemen boys and girls we are prepared for the aliens. Today what you have witnessed is more than a miracle. Today I present to you our prototype the invisibles." Suddenly a robot lost its camouflage. Marta the reporter jumped up touching her backside. "So, it, was you? You, naughty boy."

"Ladies and gentlemen, I present you with the invisibles. Look next to you now where ever you are. You might be relieving yourself I apologize for that, you might be making love to your wife or husband right now, I apologize, or most importantly you might be under attack by these aliens. I say to you all don't be afraid! The invisibles are there to protect you. You are precious to us as your leaders and to me personally. I watched our neighbors being taken away to be eaten by the aliens trust me when I say I value your privacy. Trust me when I say I value your rights to choose how you are going to die or live but what I saw these aliens do is worse than breaching your rights. Or watch you make love to your loved ones. Humanity was there and shall continue. The journey continues with us. Most have failed and will continue to fail but we shall be the first to resort to any means necessary to survive."

The Vice President paused and looked in the camera. Everyone looked among them and looked at the invisibles in each house.

"I don't know what you are thinking right now but I say to you whatever it is it can't be worse than the threat of being cooked alive and later be eaten. I will let you see the footage of what actually happened today and let you decide for yourself."

The Vice President pointed at the big screen and the camera shifted focus to the big screen. Everyone looked there. An infrared image of the Vice President appeared on the screen as she walked out of the building and outside. Suddenly outside they saw the invisibles harshly restraining the hostile aliens. As she approached close to the leader they saw him viciously struggling to free himself from the grip of around seven of the invisibles. All his alien friends are all restrained by the invisibles. The invisibles force, the leader of the aliens to kneel in front of the Vice President. The image clearly showed the leader struggling to free himself. The last image showed the face of the alien leader. The image remained paused on the screen. His face said it all. Pure and utmost evil. The background voice is the voice of the alien leader. Soon after the voice becomes more audible. The last conversation is replayed.

"What do you want?" Questioned the Vice President.

"I want you to get out of this country or else we will cook you alive and drain all your fluids out." Replied the alien leader TK.

"But this is our country, ours!"

Held the Vice President.

"We don't care. We are superior to humans. We can fly like the birds. What are humans? Just hair oil to us?"

"This is a serious matter ladies and gentlemen boys and girls. Think about this. What is more important to you today? Your life or your privacy rights? Each one of you can have his or her own invisible friend. This is the way forward. I am not going to let anyone take us to those days when aliens cooked our neighbors while we watch. Today we have a say in all this. So, it's an individual choice. You can choose to accept the invisibles or not. It's all simply. If you like the idea if you are serious about your life. Then shake the invisible right now and that's acceptance that you want to be in my program of protection. If you think that privacy matters to you the most then please open the door right now and the invisible will come back to us. There are no second chances in life so likewise it's a one of offer. The cost of running the project is in billions and the cost of the invisible to you is just a fraction of this." The Vice President paused for a while.

"This is the small print; the invisibles cost thousands of dollars and you shall pay this money as a lump sum or as installments. We have arranged several deals with banks and insurance companies so that each one of you can afford the invisibles."

Later that day the Vice President and the President are talking in the office.

"I felt embarrassed today by being snubbed by the leader of the aliens."

"Mr. President, I invested billions into this project I have more than thirty of these invisibles and you have how many?"

"Just one, that boy."

"Exactly, I told you to be part of this but guess whose side you took? Morals side, oh, my image this, my image that. I sacrificed everything, sleepless nights and all the hard work. I grabbed the bull by its horns and set up a brilliant plan. Look today we have accomplished phase ten which is ten years away from now. To answer you, what you did is what a President should do. Don't put yourself at risk unnecessarily. You, just familiarize yourself with the problem and leave it to the experts. I took this risk which most might not have taken. I am not here, to look for recognition or popularity no, that's your job. I am here to sell an idea and get paid for it. Every one of these people should be paying into this project.

"I never looked at it from that point of view Mrs. Vice President."

One sunny day, an alien was heating up immensely badly. The alien needed to be in the water. It's inside that felt exceedingly hot. Only oil will do the magic. The alien traveled the surrounding area in search of oil. It searched for humans to roast but none left. Over the years, the aliens have run havoc killing humans and draining their oils. Animals have suffered too. They traveled several places looking for oil.

Underground and in seas, oil had been depleted. What's left now is oil that is in the place where the remainder of the humans are staying outside the fortified country. All earth's oil had been extracted and deposited in the fortified. The alien was about to enter the fortified country when it fell to the ground. The electrocuting elements and all navigational signals were jammed and it couldn't fly. Outside the fortified walls the alien heated up rapidly and later exploded. Miles away a man hides between buildings and looked everywhere with every move. He took out a binocular and looked everywhere. He ducked soon after. Out of the blues something that looked like a jet plane came from nowhere at lightning speed and changed to an alien as it grabbed the man. The alien stopped and placed the man on a metal surface before touching his body and passing enormous heat through his body. Oil started dripping, out and the alien drained all the oil into its body. It repeated the process until the man's oils have all been melted. Another alien came in a flash and grabbed the man's corpse and restarted the process. Just as it absorbed the oil, other aliens arrive and the fight for the man's oil began. No natural oil and extremely hard to find human oil. The whole surrounding area humans have either escaped or ended up being cooked. At the gates of the fortified country. There are huge queues. The aliens are taking advantage of this situation, grabbing some of the people before they entered the fortified country. Those entering must be members of the $50,000 club first. Those people left outside and in the surrounding area their last hope is this country. A lot of people are outside holding guns and luggage. They are waiting for their turn. Mark looked at the poster on one of the doors the poster clearly stated that the $50,000 club will be closed in a day's time as the day after was the deadline. Mark pushed tremendously hard jumping queues and advancing forward. Knocking others down along the way. The guard came out and tried to drag Mark out of the queue after a lady complained but Mark wrestled the guard over powering him and running inside.

"Out now! You jumped the queue. Go in the queue like everyone else."

"I am inside already I am not going outside."

The guard called another guard and the two men tried to carry Mark outside but he clung to the pillar and grabbed the pillar never letting go. The guards violently kicked him very hard. Kicking him all over his body and his hands but he did not let go. He clung to the pillar and other people started entering the wall that's when they let him go. He looked at a kid holding a doll and smiled blood coming out from his noise. He pulled back tears and wiped his face. A woman on the counter inside shouted for the next customer and he stood up and walked in he looked behind him and in the air and smiled at the lady serving him.

"$50,000 Sir."

Requested the cashier lady. Mark quickly took out the money and handed it to the cashier. He looked backward as he entered through the gates. Tears dropped down his cheeks. The aliens are all on top of the sea circulating. It appears they have been there for a significantly long time. After a while they all hold still in the air above the ocean. Underneath in the ocean a huge spray of water is released into the air. As soon as the big whale fired a jet of water from its mouth, the aliens shot down into the water with lighting speeds and together carried the whale onto the rocks before electrocuting it. Huge amounts of fat started dripping down the rocks and an orgy of oil feasting began. Further up another swarm of aliens are over the ocean waters when a group of seals suddenly appeared. In a flash the aliens carried the seals onto the rocks and later they absorb the oils. None stop, soon after repeating the roasting of the whale and the seals the aliens gathered above the ocean waters. Far away in the fortified country Mark had just entered through the main gates. He saw a security guard standing on the entrance. He showed him his documents. The security officer checked all his document, and he entered inside. A totally different picture. He thought about everything he had gone through and tears simply ran down his cheeks. He stood in front of the television. An anchor-woman was reporting the news.

"A satellite image has just been released showing aliens over the ocean. It's shocking what is happening out there. These aliens have nearly caused the extinction of humans and animals like the whale as well. These were believed to be the last animals to be identified on the satellite image. All whales, gone, dolphins, gone, seals gone, I mean everything. Last week we released footage of a man who was captured at such speeds unimaginable. Although it is believed that a group of resistance is still outside the fortified country." The anchor-woman paused for a while before screaming. It's chaotic in the news the television crews and camera man are running toward the news van. They switched channels and briefly she talked again.

"This has just been received. This is happening as we speak outside the fortified country. This is a live satellite image."

The screen quickly turned to the other screen, and the screen is instantly zoomed. Mark stopped and dropped his luggage and moved closer to the screen. Without saying anything he ran out toward the gates past the security officer and looked outside through the window.

"Frank! Frank! Frank! Please open the door for my friend. Open the door please. Frank run. Frank!"

The security guards quickly looked outside and saw a swarm of aliens outside, just arriving. The people started panicking and hitting the doors shouting for the doors to be open. The security guard called another security guard. He ran toward the gate office. "Open the gate before they attack please open the gate." Pleaded Mark. The security guards looked at each other.

"We can't open the gates. It's too late now. Sorry."

"What do you mean it's too late now? They are still alive look. Let them in." Mark tried to open the gates. The security guards just watched him.

"Please what do you mean you can't?"

The security guards shoot each other a quick glance before one replied.

"If we open the gates that deactivates the signal jammers and the electric shocks."

"In other words, we will let the aliens in. Then the whole country is dead."

"So, are you saying you are going to leave them to be taken by the aliens?"

"I am afraid so. It's either them or all of us." Mark touched the mirror and Frank on the other side looking as if he had already died placed his hand too. They looked in horror as the aliens formed a circle and advanced floating in the air vertical and upside down. The greedy ones rushed to grab humans from the group of people locked outside but the lack of a signal and the electric shocks knocked the aliens down. For a while they kept seeing them falling to the ground and hearing heavy thumps until they were approaching in large numbers at the same time and some dropping down but grabbing humans down before going back. Mark cried inconsolably as Frank was grabbed.

"Fight. Fight. Fight. Fight! Fight! Frank! Frank! Oh, my God they took Frank! It was a sad scene outside. The aliens were approaching in large numbers the front group felt the whole force of the electricity and jammers but those behind grabbed the victims one by one. Frank was dragged away and laid on a slab outside and after that the aliens fought each other to absorb his oils. The security guards who had tried to throw Mark out stood behind him and apologized. Inside the fortress thrived. All the worlds oils were inside here. All the worlds money was in here, all the world's best brains and all true believers people with a dream and energy to fight for something were in this country protected by one woman; The Vice President who developed this idea and saw it through. The President opened the door and entered the Vice President's office.

"I was with the Chief of National Security today. All the satellite images show no sign of human activity on earth apart from this country. All major mammals gone. Are we going to die also?

"No Mr. President we are safe. I took this challenge

years ago after my friend argued that no woman would rule the world alone and today I am the only woman ruling the world."

"So, Mrs. Vice President you are telling me that you nearly brought the extinction of mankind just to prove that. You single handedly destroyed humanity just to prove that?"

"Oh, what are you still doing here?"

Instantly the invisible robots appeared.

"I saved you once and I destroy you today. You heard the lady; 'only the woman to rule the world'." The President touched his heart and fell to the ground.

CHAPTER THIRTEEN

A month earlier The Professor left his lab and hysterically ran upstairs to the Vice President's office. He knocked the door and for the first-time entered the office without being invited in. He looked at the Vice President breathing heavily.

"It's time Mrs. Vice President."

Declared the Professor bending down touching both his knees breathing heavily. The Vice President got up she looked like she had seen a ghost, astonished and speechless.

"Are you sure about this Professor?"

"More than sure. Phase 17 has just begun."

The Professor entered the office and sat in the comfy sofa. The Vice President walked to the window and pushed the curtain aside. She looked at the Professor her face showing mixed feelings. At one point, she showed fear and all the others triumph.

"It seemed so soon, I mean sooner than I thought. Every stage has been years earlier than planned. I need the President in here."

"This is it. It is either a do or die situation, the worst challenge mankind will face."

"This could be the end of the world. We should put everything in place. Did you double checked if we have everything ready, Professor?"

"As far as I know yes all what is left to do is in your hands."

Later they heard a sharp knock on the door and the door opening before they have even answered it.

"Is that true, it is phase 17?" asked the President breathing heavily. "I came as fast as I heard about this."

They all sat down and looked at each other. Soon after there was a knock on the door, just like the others the Chief of National Security entered the office and walked as fast as he can.

"Gentlemen what you are about to witness is something that has never been done before and I guarantee you that will never be done again." Declared the Vice President pausing for a while. She stood up and walked to the window. She breathed heavily and looked outside. She walked back and sat down.

"Phase 17 has finally arrived. I don't know what to say. We have to act extremely quick as per plan."

"What is phase 17 in layman's terms?"

Questioned the President. They all looked at each other.

"Isolation, independence, evolution and extinction of humanity. We shall be the only survivors. The list is endless starvation, riches and power.

"How do we know that we have reached this stage if I may ask." Inquired the President looking at the Vice

President. The Vice President in turn looked at the Professor. The Professor stood up and switched the projector on.

"Yesterday I checked the world's oil reserves non-left outside our border. The last known reserves showing on the map is where the aliens have assembled now. So, this is our key point one. Running out of oil all over earth. The Professor paused and looked at the Vice President.

"The aliens without the oil they will technically die. We tested their ability to think and solve simply problems and we can conclude that they will bring upon their own doom."

"Why did you say that?"

"Mr. President. The aliens since we introduced them they know very well that they rely on oil yet they brought all the world's oils to us, okay they traded with human oil one can argue but in the end how can they survive without oil?"

"That brings me to the key point number two. Lack of oil and resources will bring about starvation in all areas outside our borders. Leaving man prone to alien attack. This can lead to human extinction. Aliens developed a taste of human oil. When natural oil is, all contained in our country, the aliens will deplete humans outside our fortress."

The Professor paused.

"That brings me to point number three isolation. With immediate effect, we should start the process of isolation. Our country should be fortified. We shall advertise the $50 000 club entry option for a limited time after that no one should enter. That takes me to the key point four; this is the influx of people and resources money and skills we will need. Only people

who can be part of the $50,000 club will be allowed. After that we will have our borders fortified. We shall make entry hard and instill deterrents on all borders that will hinder aliens entering. Any aliens who enters dies here. We will put signal jammers so that aliens stay outside. You might be wondering why this is because they might end up killing us too. The Professor now looked at the Vice President.
"Yes, this last stage is the highly crucial stage. It's a challenge for aliens. What can one do to survive when oil runs out? The aliens will lead us to another planet where there is oil. If they don't evolve, they will die.

CHAPTER FOURTEEN

A plane hovers over a long stretch of land and buildings. In fact, it had flown several areas without noticing any major life activities. The Professor was with the Vice President.

"It's just our country left, we have to start rebuilding. Start again. New start new beginnings. Give each person in our country their own small kingdom. Earth has given us a second chance, a new hope all races, everyone. The world was being destroyed by crooks, lazy people, evil people, too much corruption, unnecessary killings, all bad people. The people in my country today are people with a vision. People who reminds me of my younger self. People who fight for something. Visionaries, the leaders of tomorrow, people who believe to be successful you must emit success yourself."

"I agree with you. The world needed someone like you. A visionary, a woman of substance."

Raising a glass of wine.

"To new beginnings, a new honest world. A world of dreams and hopes. A world full of honest, loyal and hardworking people."

"But Mrs. Vice President, I think you have to redo all this again?"

"Professor what makes you say that?"

"Human nature I guess. Soon these people will be corrupt again. It's just human nature. Even now I still can't understand humans."

"Now Professor you see why I favored aliens to humans?"

"Aliens oh, our greatest cleaners."

Soon after there is a warning message being announce.

"Please remain seated and fasten your seat-belts. Possible alien activity," advised the pilot.

"I thought you said that you deactivated all the aliens?" Inquired the Vice President looking at the Professor scared and worried.

"This is the first-time I have seen you scared and worried Mrs. Vice President. JT is cleaning up making sure he collects all the chips from the aliens for safe keeping before storing them. Like I said we might need these again in our lifetime."

"Did TK return from Mars?"

The Professor looked astonished.

"You sent TK to Mars? Why?"

"Oil, Professor oil."

"Look at this satellite image Mrs. Vice President."

"What is it?" asked the Vice President looking at huge mass graves in former oil reserve sites.

"So, that is where all the aliens were burying the dead?"

"Oil, Mrs. Vice President, oil."

The plane flew past an alien.
"Is that TK I have just seen?" Quizzed the Professor.
"So, there is oil on mars? Maybe we will still need the aliens after all," suggested the Vice President.

THE END